Shadows of Winterbury

A Victorian Era Vampire Tale

Gerilyn Marin

*This one is for the readers who encouraged
me to stretch beyond my comfort zone.
Thank you for believing that I could.*

Contents

Portraying the Victorian Era

This was written in the spirit of simple, spooky entertainment. It captures the essence I recall from watching period horror/dramas as a child (some of which I can only remember bits & pieces of to this day), since the tale occured to me set in the Victorian Era.

I already knew some information on the period, and did *some* research (imagine my surprise that wristwatches were worn exclusively by women as a fashion accessory, hence pocket watches for men). As such, I feel the need to forewarn readers there may be some historical inaccuracies. I kindly ask that should you stumble across any, take them with a grain of salt.

That being said, I *know* some readers are sticklers for accuracy. I figured I would prefer to put this note here, where it can be read in the Amazon/ Kindle shop prior to purchase, permitting readers to make an informed decision, and sparing anyone who might be taken out of the story over errors on my part.

Chapter One

A Fortunate Meeting

"**C**lifford, Douglas! Please don't run off!"

Violet sighed, shaking her head as the Devitt boys bolted through the park. Honestly, it was as though they heard *do* in the place of every *don't*.

Her mahogany eyes rolling heavenward, she pleaded silently for this day to be over, already. Drawing a deep breath, she winced at the strain against the bones of her new corset. She gathered her skirts in her hands and hurried after them.

The boys stopped by the grand fountain in

the center of the park. At least they were in her eye-line, she considered, as she permitted herself to stop after just a few yards.

The only thing to keep her from doubling over as she fought to catch her breath was the stiffness of her dress and the dreadful pinch of her aforementioned corset. Tipping back her head, she brushed some loose strands of her naturally frenzied reddish-brown hair out of her eyes—it had been all neat and tidy when Mr. Devitt had suggested she escort the boys to the park, as they were *too bored* at the party.

Now she was certain chasing after them had turned her locks into a puffy ball of madness atop her head.

Sparing a moment, she ran the fingers of her lace-gloved hands over her hair. Her shoulders drooped in relief as she found that only those few tendrils had gone wayward from her coiled, perfectly ordered chignon.

She started along the cobblestone path once more, but slowed her pace almost immediately. There was an odd, fleeting sensation against her back, as though someone stood close behind her.

Brow furrowing, she turned her head to look over her shoulder. The path was entirely empty; the only other visitors were too far from her to have caused the strange feeling.

Frowning, she put the incident out of her head and quickened her steps again to hurry after the boys as she turned her attention forward. She never saw the gentleman rushing along in her direction until they collided.

Violet lost her footing. Stumbling, she gashed her knee against a broken stone in the path. She looked up, trying not to let her eyes water as the pain seared across her skin.

"I'm so sorry," they said at the same time, their voices mingling.

She froze, feeling her cheeks warm a little as she met his blue-eyed gaze. Though, she did wonder what was fascinating him so as he stared back at *her*, his full lips parting ever so slightly as he drew in a sharp breath.

He blinked a few times in rapid succession before he shook his head, appearing to regain his bearings. "No, no. *I* apologize, my lady," he said, offering one leather-gloved hand to her as he pressed the other over his heart in a show of sincerity.

Her brows shot up as she slipped her fingers into his. That finely-tailored dark suit and the way he carried himself.... She thought for certain he'd be demanding that she watch her step more carefully next time, not offering words of contrition.

Perhaps her present state of dress had him fooled into thinking she was of higher station than a governess—at this moment, she had all the airs of an aristocrat's daughter. Words of gratitude for his assistance stuck in her throat as she allowed him to pull her to her feet.

Heat lanced her knee as she moved and she let out a hissing breath. Violet hobbled a little to one side as she attempted to get a look at the injury whilst also trying not to lean on him as she did so.

"Oh, dear," he said, shaking his head. "Come, sit." The mysterious gentleman slipped his free hand around her elbow as he guided her toward the fountain.

She must've been dazed from her tumble, she thought, because before she knew it, she found herself seated on a nearby bench. Though, she could still hear Clifford and Douglas playing, which calmed her somewhat—she had feared the clever boys would have taken advantage of her distraction just now and darted off again—she couldn't seem to stop staring at the man's face.

His hair fell in neat, dark waves, contrasting his bright eyes and fair skin. There was the barest dusting of color in his high-boned cheeks, yet she didn't know if that was from the sun, or perhaps embarrassment at causing her injury.

To her shock, he knelt before her. He appeared to think through what he was doing only *after* he started, his fingers gently touching the hem of her skirts.

"May I have a look at it?"

A blush flooded her cheeks instantly and she snapped her head around, glancing about the park. It was all fine and well that he wanted to make sure the wound was not severe, but she suddenly feared some passerby misunderstanding the situation.

"I . . . ." She chewed her lip as she shook her head. "I don't think that's—"

"Please?" His dark, perfectly arched brows drew upward as he offered her a charming grin. "I *do* have some medical knowledge, and I would be ever so grateful if you would permit me to see to your injury."

Ever so grateful? Her jaw dropped a little as she stared back at him. "All right," she said, her voice lower than she intended, "if you're going to insist so."

That grin melted down to a serene half-smile as he nodded and carefully pushed back her skirts. He held in an endeared chuckle at the way she stiffened as he brushed gentle fingertips over the tear in her stocking around the cut. Such wonderful innocence.

"I am sorry to say that I ruined your hose."

The girl didn't answer. He looked up to see how she eyed her skirts. She sniffled, and there was the faintest glimmer of wetness on her dark, curled lashes.

"I'm sorry," he said again, darting his gaze back to the gash. Surely the wound *was* a bit impressive for how narrow it was, but he didn't think it enough to bring her to tears. "Does it hurt that badly?"

"No, it's not that." It didn't exactly tickle, but she was long used to little pains like this, though she didn't bear scars in evidence of that—she'd always been a quick healer, so whatever pain injuries brought never lasted long.

Folding her lips inward, she smoothed her hands over the top layer of her skirts. The butter-yellow fabric was torn and stained with drops of crimson. "I've ruined my dress. My—my uncle bought it for me, and *now* its ruined."

He spoke as he retrieved a silk handkerchief from inside his jacket to gently dab at her cut. "You should allow me to compensate you for the cost."

"That's very kind, but I couldn't possibly ask that of you." She shrugged as she managed to tear her gaze from him to look toward the boys. They had busied themselves sword fighting with sticks.

"Clifford, Douglas! Will you *please* be careful? You're going to put someone's eye out!"

As she turned back, she couldn't miss how his attention flicked in the direction of the children before returning to her. "Aren't those the Devitt boys?"

Violet nodded, her gaze on the horizon a moment as she confessed, "I'm their governess."

He bit his lip but remained silent. How sweet that she thought it an embarrassing revelation to admit her station to him.

"Are you friends of the family?" She didn't know why she asked, perhaps to fill the sudden silence—if he were a friend, wouldn't he be at the party now?

"No," he said, his expression thoughtful as he tipped his head, presumably examining the cut. "I know of them only by name, really. We travel in the same circles, I suppose you could say."

"I see." She remained polite, a small smile plucking at the corners of her mouth, but she had the feeling he was actually a bit *above* the Devitt's circles. It was nice to think he didn't want to intimidate her with whatever his true standing was.

"I believe I'd heard that they're moving abroad?"

Her brows pinched together as she met his gaze, again. He'd seen to her cut, and now knew the discussion was probably not worth his time. Why, then, did she feel as though he was making excuses to carry on their conversation?

"Yes. Today is their farewell party." She hurried on, supplying him more information than was asked to see if he was only curious, or was—as mad as it seemed—simply interested in continuing to speak with her. "They depart in a few days."

He arched a brow. "But you won't be accompanying them?"

Shaking her head, she fussed with her skirts, pushing them back down into place.

"That will leave you unemployed, then?"

My, he certainly was the inquisitive sort. The handsome gentleman's unwavering attention was beginning to make her bashful.

Violet shrugged, forcing her expression to remain neutral as best she could. "I'm certain the agency will find me something."

"Yes," he said as he nodded. "I'm certain they *will.*"

"We want to go home, now."

Clifford's voice at her shoulder gave Violet a start. She turned, glancing from Clifford to Douglas, and back.

"Tuckered yourselves out, have you?"

Douglas pouted. "No! We're hungry."

"I suppose I should be on my way, as well."

Violet looked to the gentleman as he rose to his feet. He held his hand out to her, his gaze on hers, all the while. She slipped he fingers into his, as she had a few minutes earlier, and allowed him to assist her to stand.

"Are you certain you won't allow me to compensate you for the dress?"

"I couldn't." She extracted her hand from his in a delicate gesture—he seemed to have forgotten he was holding her. "My uncle wouldn't want—"

"Can we see Hugh again before we take ship?"

Violet frowned, her expression stern as she looked to the shorter of the two fair-haired boys. "Douglas! You know it's rude to interrupt adult conversation." When the boy looked abashed, her features softened. "I'm sorry, but you know my uncle is a terribly busy man. He's preparing for a concert as we speak . . . . However, I *will* ask him."

"Concert? Is your uncle by any chance Hugh Sinnet, the violinist?"

She appreciated that he didn't state Hugh's full moniker. The *Mad* Violinist was more an affectionate title than a statement of his demeanor—though she did often think he might be at least a *little* mad—due to his obvious passion as he played. His long, jet curls swung this way and that in frenzied motions, so by the end of any performance, he did indeed look *quite* mad. A number of critics even compared him to Paganini.

"Yes. You know of him?"

"I am quite familiar with his work. I went to hear him play last month in London." The man furrowed his brow as his gaze searched her face, but then he shook his head. "I'm sorry. I knew he had a brother who passed on; I suppose I'm trying to look for a family resemblance."

"Oh, no," she said, casting her gaze downward before meeting his eyes, once more. "I'm not Larkin's daughter. Hugh was a friend of the family, and when my parents passed, he took me in. I was young at the time, and was raised with his nephew, and . . . ."

He was staring at her so intently as she spoke that the words caught in her throat. Why on earth was she babbling at him like this?

Violet shrugged, shaking her head and forcing a gulp down her throat. "Naturally, he always addressed Hugh as *Uncle*, so I started to as well," she finished, her voice small.

"My name is Ives," the gentleman said, seeming uttlery enchanted by her flustered state. Smiling, he gently took her hand in his and pressed a kiss to the back before letting it drop, again. "At the very least, you may tell your uncle you met one of his admirers today."

There was a strange rush of relief and disappointment as she recognized that he was *actually* taking his leave, now.

"My name is Violet. It was a pleasure speaking with you, Ives. Thank you for your kind assistance."

"Miss Ramsey, *c'mon*," Clifford whined.

Her frame slumped as she took each of the boys' hands in hers. "Yes, yes. We *are* going, I was only . . . ." Her voice trailed off as she looked up again to find Ives nowhere in sight. ". . . Being polite."

She furrowed her brow as she looked along the path. "Did either of you boys see where the gentleman disappeared to?"

They both shrugged and shook their heads in response.

Something on the ground snagged her attention. She bent to retrieve the scrap of pale fabric, realizing as she picked it up that the gentleman'd dropped his handkerchief.

Turning it over, she ran a fingertip over the initials embroidered into the white silk. "I.H.?"

Chapter Two

Under the Guise of Trust

Ives watched the girl depart, her young charges in tow.

He truly hadn't intended to carry on the conversation as long as he had. Yet, the longer she spoke, the more he wanted her to keep speaking. The color in her cheeks, the flecks of dark crimson in her brown eyes. The sweet line of her cleavage over the top of her dress, and how her breasts shivered as she had fidgeted in place, fussing over her skirts.

A half-grin playing on his lips, he looked to

the drops of crimson on his finger. Fishing a small vial from his pocket, he uncorked it and carefully scraped some of the steadily-cooling liquid into it. Of course, it would be cold by the time he got it home, but there was little to be done for it.

Replacing the stopper, Ives lapped the remnants from the leather of his glove. He bit hard into his bottom lip as his eyelids drifted downward.

Yes, he'd suspected this the moment he caught the scent of her blood. And she was a ward of the Sinnet family?

That *was* fortunate, indeed.

"Violet Ramsey," he said in a whisper, opening his eyes to watch her, once more—she was nearly out of his line of sight, now. "You really are a perfect creature, aren't you?"

He inspected the blood inside the glass for a moment. "And I'm certain *he* will prove it so."

And Three Weeks Later

"Still nothing?" Fletcher asked over lunch.

Violet looked up from her meal and shrugged. She played with her utensils, but didn't have much of an appetite just now. "I've checked the post *every* day. I don't know. Perhaps the Devitts gave me a bad reference."

"Rubbish." He shook his head, though he seemed rather absorbed in eating as he spoke. His lack of etiquette made her sigh, despite that it was a somewhat of an adorable trait to which she was well accustomed. "You're a fantastic teacher, and Grace says you are *amazing* with her nieces."

Violet strained to keep her eyes from rolling. She adored Grace, but this was not the time for Fletcher to take yet another opportunity to fawn over his fiancée.

"I don't know," she said again. "Grace's practically family. She could only be doing me a kindness by saying such things."

"Violet," Hugh called as he stepped into the dining room. "You have a tele—"

"Oh, *thank* you!" She was out of her chair and across the room so fast, Fletcher swore he blinked and missed her movements.

She all but snatched the telegram from Hugh's hand, bouncing on the balls of her feet as she opened it.

Hugh watched her as she read the message. It didn't escape Fletcher's notice that his uncle looked . . . nervous, somehow. He couldn't quite put his finger on it.

"It's a position in the country! I'm requested as governess at Winterbury Hall? Where is . . . ?" Her voice trailed off as she noted the name of her prospective employer. "The home of Lord Ives Hayward, the Second?"

I.H.? That charming—if rather intense—gentleman from the park? Well, he had known she would be out of work now, and had her full name on account of Clifford's impatient wailing.

Had Ives.... *Hayward,* Lord *Ives Hayward, the Second,* she corrected herself, requested her, especially?

She didn't know if the giddiness in her stomach was relief after thinking she might not find work any time soon, or something brought on by the thought of seeing him again. The latter part she ignored, for—*as* her employer—that was quite an inappropriate reaction for her to have toward him.

Her eyebrows lifted as she looked up from the message. "I'm expected to arrive by this evening! Oh, I must go pack my trunk."

Hugh smiled as she bounced up to plant on a kiss on his cheek. While she pivoted on her heel and dashed up the stairs, Fletcher observed how Hugh's cheerful expression melted, leaving behind a pained grimace.

He opened his mouth to ask, but his uncle was already walking out of the room. After a moment, he heard the grating of metal against stone.

Brow furrowing, he pushed back his chair and stood. "Uncle Hugh?"

By the time Fletcher reached the sitting room, Hugh was kneeling before the fireplace. He'd pulled away the screen and was watching something in the flames.

"Uncle? What are you doing?"

Hugh shot to his feet as he jerked his head around to look at Fletcher. "Nothing," he said, swallowing hard as he shook his head.

"It clearly *isn't* nothing." Fletcher stormed across the room to see for himself. In the fire, he could make out the blackened curling of paper . . . . Here and there, lettering. He was able to piece together enough words to understand what he was seeing.

"Telegrams from Violet's agency?" Fletcher glanced over his shoulder at his uncle, his throat so tight with anger he wasn't certain he could get the words out. "She's been going mad for *weeks* believing no one wanted to employ her! Why would you do this?"

Hugh only shook his head again, his grey eyes watering as he stared into the fire.

Fletcher followed the man's gaze. He saw one paper, different from the rest—a letter that had yet to be wholly swallowed by the flames.

"Fletcher, *don't*," Hugh said, even as the younger man bent and snatched the letter from the hearth.

Frowning, Fletcher waved the paper gently to extinguish the burning edges. Ice churned in the pit of his stomach as he read aloud what was left. "... *Ramsey. Deliver her and the debt of the Sinnet family shall be considered paid in full. Yours, I.H.*.."

His brows drew upward and he shook his head in disbelief. Lord Ives Hayward, II, as Violet'd read from her new *employer's* request. Forcing a gulp down his throat, Fletcher looked to the fireplace, the remnants of the telegrams now nothing but ash, and then to Hugh.

"I don't understand." He paused a moment to force a breath, his voice thick. "Uncle, what have you done?"

With a mirthless grin, Hugh took the smoldering paper from his nephew's hand and put it back in the flames. Straightening up, he shook his head, a tear escaping to roll down his cheek.

After a moment of attempting to compose himself, he finally said, "I've protected you *and* your fiancée." *And your future children*, but he left that unsaid, assuring himself that Lord Hayward, and his so-called ward would treat Violet well.

Before Fletcher could inquire about this last part, Hugh turned sharply and clamped his hands over Fletcher's shoulders. "Whatever you think, you mustn't say a word. For your own sake, *and* Violet's."

Fletcher didn't *know* what to think as he looked from his uncle to the ceiling. He could only imagine how excited Violet was as she fluttered about on the floor above their heads.

Packing to leave for Winterbury Hall ....

But he couldn't stop wondering. Debt? What debt? Since when did the Sinnet family owe any*thing* to any*one*? He was even less certain now about what was happening than he'd been a moment ago. Unless . . . .

Exactly how old was this debt the Lord was claiming? And *why* was Hugh honoring it?

He knew Hugh wouldn't give him an answer, but Fletcher suddenly had a suspicion.

Old tales from childhood awoke in the back of his mind. *Dark* tales. Things he dared never mention to Violet. She always said she didn't have time for superstition, less so for the possibility of inhuman things.

Even if they were things that—if they existed— might be in a position to hold sway over families like his thanks to some long-forgotten promise, grudge, or debt.

He felt obligated to respect Uncle's wish not to tell Violet of whatever this was, but he would write her every week, he decided—every day, if need be—to make sure she kept safe. And the *moment* he thought she might be in danger, he'd go to Winterbury Hall and retrieve her, himself. Uncle Hugh's caution be damned.

The words fell from Fletcher's lips, low, yet thick and clumsy. "Will we ever see her again?"

Hugh met his nephew's gaze, his voice slipping out in barely audible whisper as he shook his head. "I wish I knew."

Chapter Three

Her New Employers

Violet bit her lip as she watched the land-scape drifting by beyond the window. She'd barely been traveling two hours, yet already she missed her family. This was the first time she'd been offered a position so very far from home.

Fletcher had trailed her every step so closely as she finished packing, and after taking her trunk down to the carriage for her, that she wouldn't be wholly surprised if she found him hiding in her things when she finally arrived at Winterbury Hall. It broke her heart a little, though, that after a single quick hug—so tight it stole her breath a moment—Uncle Hugh hadn't seen her off.

Her shoulders drooped and she sniffled as she wondered if she'd done something to upset him.

"No, Violet," she whispered to herself as she shook her head, blinking rapidly to keep any possible tears at bay. "He was simply too upset to see you off, because you're going so far away. Nothing to fuss about."

Forcing a smile, she looked out the window, once more. The sky was darkening as the sun set in the distance and the trees lining the road had thickened from sparse, but scenic wedges of foliage to true, full woods sooner than she'd noticed.

She swallowed hard as she watched the last bits of pink-tinged clouds sink lower against the horizon. Dear God, why had that telegram arrived so late? She could have made this journey *hours* earlier and been safely ensconced within her new employer's home, by now.

With no explanation for the delay, she only hoped Ives—Hayward, she reminded herself, the tone of her inner-voice one of admonishment—*Lord* Hayward would not consider her late arrival a mark against her.

Fretting as she was, she didn't notice the carriage slowing until she felt the rumble of its wheels whilst they rolled to a stop beneath her. A sudden chill ran along her skin under the sleeves of her dress and the pit of her stomach twisted into a knot.

Perhaps if she could know he wouldn't hold her responsible for the time of her arrival, she would be far less nervous.

She rolled her eyes at herself and shook her head. Perhaps if she hadn't thought him so handsome when they'd first met—an observation now made wholly inappropriate by her new position as his employee—she would be far less nervous.

After all, he was hiring a *governess*; she doubted *Lady* Hayward would take kindly to how Violet had clearly read too much into his attention during their conversation in that park those weeks ago.

She jumped a little as the driver opened her door. There she went, getting caught up in her own thoughts, again.

Violet nodded, smiling politely as he held out a hand to help her from the carriage. Climbing down, taking in the main house of the sprawling, foreboding grounds, ascending the curving front steps . . . even watching numbly as the driver pulled the bell, and then returned to the carriage to retrieve her trunk, all passed in a blur.

Swallowing hard, she squared her shoulders and once more plastered on a sweet grin as the fine, polished double-doors before her creaked open. A mousy-looking little man in an immaculate butler's uniform stood inside, eyeing her cautiously.

When he said nothing—no *Good evening*, no *May I help you*, unsettling Violet, quite frankly, with his lack of greeting—she forced her smile brighter and nodded as she said, "Good evening, sir. I am—"

"Violet Ramsey."

She bit her lip against the giddy rush that zipped through her at the sound of Lord Hayward's well-remembered voice saying her name. Drat it, she would *really* have to keep that in check.

Lord Hayward swept up behind the smaller man, just as devastatingly handsome as she recalled. "Now, Gilbert, do not be rude. This young lady is here at my invitation."

Gilbert bowed his head. "My apologies, Lord —"

The Lord wagged a finger at him. "Gilbert, please. I *have* asked you not to call me that."

Again, the little man capitulated. "Of course . . . Ives." Though, in Violet's view, Gilbert didn't seem quite comfortable addressing their employer so informally.

"Take Violet's trunk up to the room your prepared earlier, would you?"

Desperate not to have to address the Lord by anything that would feel problematic again, the girl thought, Gilbert merely nodded and hurried to take her things. Frowning, she turned to observe him.

"I'm afraid it's actually quite heavy. There

were books I couldn't leave behind. Perhaps someone should help—"

"It's fine, but your concern is warming," Lord Hayward said with a grin. "I assure you, Gilbert is stronger than he looks. He'll manage."

Nodding, Violet watched, her eyes going wide as Gilbert indeed hefted the trunk as though it were filled with feathers. She backpedaled, allowing him to make his way through the door. Without realizing she was moving, she crossed the threshold into the foyer to observe the man as he toddled through the ground floor and then started up the staircase, never taking even a moment's pause.

Only when he disappeared beyond her field of vision, did she notice that she'd entered the house. More alarming, still, that she stood *quite* close beside Lord Hayward without his invitation!

She turned and backed away until she was a respectable distance from him. She also ignored that he seemed quietly amused by her reaction to his nearness.

"Please forgive my forwardness, Lord Hayward," Violet said, offering a curtsy.

When she looked up, she found him responding to the formal gesture with a dismissive wave as he shook his head. "Please, Violet. I shall tell you as you just heard me tell Gilbert, call me Ives."

She was a bit startled by his improper manner, vehemently ignoring that she liked the way her name sounded rolling off his tongue. "I don't believe such informality is appropriate with one's employer, Sir. After all, what might *Lady* Hayward think of you addressing your governess so?"

His brow furrowed, seeming as though he had issue untangling her words. After a stammering heartbeat, he let out a surprised chuckle. "Oh, I see. No, no. There are some things concerning your post that must be discussed before I introduce you to your charge. The first . . . there *is* no Lady Hayward. And before wondering if I'm widowed, no. There never was a Lady Hayward."

Violet opened her mouth to inquire further on this point, but already he was turning on his heel to start toward the wide staircase that led up to a second level, and at least one more floor beyond. With a sobering shake of her head, she hurried to catch up to his long-legged stride.

"The second is that we are so very isolated here—as you likely realized from your journey to the estate, I'm sure—that a bit of informality is not of consequence." A bemused half-smile curved his lips as he glanced over his shoulder at her. "Indeed, you'll find some days it helps you retain your sanity."

She smiled in spite of herself; there was just something about his presence that overwhelmed her. Unsettling, yes, but not nearly enough to alarm her—just the strange impression of wanting to smile when he smiled, laugh when he laughed.

Perhaps he was simply infectious that way, as some people were.

The sound of thunder rumbling outside the walls drew her focus a moment. She frowned as she looked toward the nearest window. Certainly, she'd noticed a few clouds gathering when she'd stepped from the carriage, but nothing to denote imminent rainfall.

When she returned her gaze to Ives, it was to find he'd also allowed himself to be distracted by the change in the weather. His blue eyes narrowed as he shook his head before snapping his attention back to her.

"Thirdly," he said, as though there'd been no interruption to his list, "I must explain some things about your student prior to your meeting him. Cassius is a . . . unique case. As such, there were matters I was unable to disclose in my communication with your agency, for reasons you'll understand once—"

"I take it this is she?"

The low-pitched voice from the second-floor landing startled her. Violet looked up only to realize herself trapped by the eyes of the man who had appeared there. She wondered, briefly, if he might not be Ives' brother. They had the same basic features—dark brown hair that fell in waves, blue eyes, strong jawlines, and appeared of similar height and build. Yet, there was no true resemblance between them.

She found herself—perhaps inappropriately, depending upon who this was—prompted to speak. "Who—?"

"Honestly, Cassius," Ives said, his tone short in a way that caused Violet to jump. "I told you to give me time to explain the situation!"

Cassius? But hadn't he only just said ... ?

In that instant, she did not care about propriety, or losing the only post she'd been offered in weeks. She only cared that she seemed to be at the heart of some sick joke.

She looked from one man to the other, and back. "One of you had better explain this, *immediately*."

Ives' brows drew upward at her fiery tone. He and Cassius exchanged a glance. And after all that insufferable insistence on propriety. Well, she *was* an interesting little thing now, wasn't she?

Ives held up his hands in a placating gesture. "Of course, of course. I was *trying* to explain until we were so rudely interrupted," he said.

At the barely-veiled admonishment, Cassius lowered his eyes and set his jaw, but remained silent.

Violet lifted her brows in expectation as she waited. She tried to ignore another rumble of thunder from outside, followed by the sudden, steady pattering of rain against the windows.

It was night and now the weather had turned. Whatever he was about to say didn't so much matter, she was trapped in this house with them at least until morning, when transportation back to Ebbing's Field could be arranged.

And she could tell from the way each man flicked his gaze toward the windows at the sound that they were equally aware of her predicament. She supposed it was a good sign, then, that Ives continued on with his explanation as though time were of the essence.

"My father was already quite old when I was born, my mother had passed on shortly after my birth from illness." Ives shook his head, his face carefully blank. "Her last wish was that I not be alone. Father, for a near-decade, refused to grant it. Cassius' family, the Vaughns, had been father's only friends—he was a very difficult man. But, when Cassius' parents died unexpectedly, father took him in, formally adopting him into our family."

Violet glanced at Cassius. His attention still on the toes of his own shoes, he'd turned and started down the staircase on slow, measured steps.

That was all *very* unfortunate, but none of it explained what was happening!

Ives tipped back his head, eyeing the ceiling as he uttered a mirthless chuckle. "Cassius was . . . sickly when we were younger. He couldn't even leave his room, let alone the house. Attempts to bring in tutors failed, as he was often too tired to pay attention for very long, at all. Being a little older, I've always been a bit protective of him. So, when my father died, I took on the responsibility of caring for him."

She refused to let her expression lighten.

Sighing, Ives let his broad shoulders slump. "Only recently did he recover from the toll of his illness. He is quite intelligent, you'll find, but he lacks formal education for obvious reasons. This is where you come in. Whenever I was honest about the position's requirements, my request for a tutor was either denied, or those who accepted left within a matter of days, unable to manage his ... unpredictable temperament."

"Unpredictable temperament?" Violet echoed, wide-eyed. *That* did not sound promising.

"Please understand, these tutors came here to teach a grown man, and thus expected the temperament of a grown man," Ives said, frowning. "As stated, he is quite intelligent, but formal lessons are a concept with which he is unaccustomed, and thus he becomes easily frustrated with them."

"And he especially dislikes being discussed as though he's *not* in the room."

At Cassius' voice so close behind her, Violet jumped nearly as much as she had when Ives had snapped at the other man only moments ago. She darted her gaze over her shoulder to see that he'd reached the foot of the stairs and come to stand with them.

She'd not even heard his footfalls.

When she turned her attention back to Ives, he was shaking his head at Cassius, the faintest scowl marring his features. "After so many failings trying to find a suitable tutor to aid him," he said, snapping his gaze back to lock on Violet's, "I realized that he needs someone capable of handling such behavior. When I recalled seeing you so patient with the Devitt boys, I realized we did not simply need a tutor, we needed a governess. However, had I revealed to your agency that I required a governess to tend a grown man . . . well, I'm certain you can appreciate why such a thing might be problematic."

Her expression softened then. There was no way not to feel sorry for their predicament.

"We hoped that if you came here, learned of the situation firsthand, you might give the offered post more serious consideration. He would need to learn all you can teach him. Etiquette, art, mathematics, history . . . he's literate, and quite a proficient reader, so perhaps that is to your advantage?"

When she was silent for a few heartbeats, and seemed in no hurry to offer a response, Cassius spoke up, his tone plucking strangely at her heart.

"Do you think you can help me?"

Chapter Four

Against Better Judgment

Violet drew a deep breath and let it out slow. She wasn't certain accepting this post was wise, but then she knew if she didn't accept, they might not find anyone willing to even entertain aiding them.

She shook her head as she turned to face the younger man. "I don't know. I need a little time to think this over." Just as the last word left her lips, she wobbled in place, the room spinning around her.

Cassius steadied her with a gentle hand on

her arm, a worried expression pinching his features. Ives moved up behind her, his fingers curling around her shoulder.

"Are you all right?" Ives asked, a note of concern in his voice.

Giving her head a shake—that only made things worse—she frowned and blinked hard. "Sorry, I just got dizzy a moment."

The men exchanged a glance before Ives went on. "Probably your long carriage ride here coupled with the shock we just gave you. Entirely our fault."

Seeming to contribute to the conversation, the rain picked up, hammering the windows fiercely.

Ives shifted to turn Violet just enough so that she was looking at both him and Cassius. "You should probably lie down. That storm and the late hour are not in your favor. There is already a room set for you, so rest, think over what we're asking of you. If, in the morning, you decline the post, I will make arrangements to see you back to your uncle's home immediately."

Again, she blinked hard, trying to get her bearings. That sounded quite reasonable, under the circumstances.

She must've nodded, she realized, as before she was really aware she was even moving, Ives had taken one arm, Cassius the other. They guided her up the staircase to the second-floor and along the left wing of the enormous house.

She didn't notice much of the décor up here, just now. She was far too focused on trying to keep her feet under her, while also attempting not to pay any mind to the press of them on either side of her.

Good Lord, when had her thoughts become so easily wayward?

Violet was drawn to a halt as Ives stepped around her to push open a door. After a cautious moment of assuring themselves she could manage on her own, they each relinquished their hold on her.

"Should you require anything during the night," Ives said, pointing down the opposite end of the corridor, "our rooms are in that wing, there. Gilbert's room is adjacent to the kitchen . . . oh, drat. We did not have the chance to give you a tour. All right, well, we are right down there, should you need anything at all. Sleep well."

Nodding, she stepped into her room. The last thing she glimpsed as she closed the door was the blue eyes of Cassius Vaughn. She didn't know him from Adam, and so she could not help but wonder if it made sense that she thought he looked impossibly sad. Some people wore miserable expressions all the time—perhaps that was simply his face.

Strangely, she could not stop herself. Pressing her hand to the door, Violet leaned close, listening. She heard their footfalls retreating to the wing Ives had indicated as containing their rooms.

"She's going to say no." Cassius' voice was a low tumble of sound that she just barely heard— sad to match his expression.

"You don't know that," Ives said, gentle and reassuring, that shortness from earlier vanished entirely.

Cassius said something she could not quite make out then, but whatever it was tore at her a little, as it somehow sounded even more dejected.

"Don't think that way. Maybe she'll surprise you. Now, you get some rest, as well."

That was the last she heard from either of them before the sound of a door closing reached her.

Violet drew a steadying breath as she pulled back, allowing her body to sag a little. Now that she was here, she had to admit she *was* quite tired.

Turning to take in her room, she felt her jaw fall, as though the response were independent of her. It was all so lovely . . . four-post bed, vanity table, writing desk set beneath a large window. There were shelves thoughtfully empty for books or knick-knacks she might've brought from home —she was certain, as another series of shelves directly across from it looked packed. She could imagine poor Gilbert, scrambling to precisely place everything from both sets of shelves in one location. It was still hard to imagine that not a single maid attended such a large house, but perhaps with only himself and Cassius to look after, Lord

Ives Hayward, II had thought the excess of more servants unnecessary.

Of course, he'd be correct in her opinion, she was simply unaccustomed to those of his station not taking luxury wherever life offered it to them.

She tried to imagine them in here—Ives giving direction as Gilbert puttered across the floor, this way and that to bring his employer's vision to life—setting the room in a way they imagined she'd find both useful and appealing. The writing desk already had a set of fine stationary and a collection of pens in the open, set beside a gorgeous lamp.

With a shake of her head, she reprimanded herself for being so taken by the prettiness and perfection of her room. No, if she was going to agree when she awoke in the morning—or decline the post if she felt the task impossible—she was going to have to come to that decision because she wanted to help Cassius, *not* because she fancied the notion of penning poetry by a window that overlooked the gardens!

"Just *rest*, Violet," she admonished herself in a hissing whisper.

Retrieving her nightclothes from her trunk, she washed up in the en-suite bathroom and changed for bed. She hated to admit that there was something sinful and luxurious about laying in that bed, with its plush quilt and fine silk pillows in her simple cotton nightdress.

But, sooner than she could remind herself—

exactly as she had in regard to the pleasing comfort and aesthetics of her room—not to let anything so frivolous weigh on her decision, she was already drifting to sleep.

∞∞∞

Violet stirred at the sweet, unfamiliar sensation of lips against her throat. Blinking open her eyes, she found herself sitting up on the edge of her bed. Her head was tipped back and she angled her gaze. A dark head was bent over her, blue eyes capturing hers briefly before they drifted closed, focusing on the kisses he was brushing against her pulse.

The dull, impossibly slow thud of his heart against her back was strangely calming.

The touch of fingers along her leg drew her attention and she found another man on his knees before her. The night-dark of the room obscured his features just enough that she did not easily recognize him —dark hair, blue eyes, just like the man who cradled her body with his own.

Those blue eyes flicked over her before he moved close. Parting her legs with gentle fingers, he pressed near to her.

Violet gasped as he captured her mouth in an eager kiss. But all too soon, it seemed, he broke away. He shifted downward against her, dragging his teeth along her body through the cotton of her nightdress.

The hands of the man holding her slipped upward as the other man lowered. She presssed her lips together, stifling a moan as he cupped her breasts, circling the tips of his fingers over her nipples.

"Oh, God," she said in a loud whisper, shuddering at the unexpected press of fingers between her thighs. She was certain she heard muffled chuckling in response to her startled cry.

But there was no time for her alarm to take root. The pressure of his fingertips became rhythmic and insistent. She could swear he murmured something soothing just before she felt his lips caressing her inner thigh.

At her throat, too, the kisses became hungrier, more urgent. The raking of his teeth against the soft flesh was delicious, as was the working of his hands as he teased her breasts further, still.

The one before her snapped up his gaze, those blue eyes catching hers as his fingers worked her harder.

Violet didn't know what had come over her—she knew she should stop this, but didn't want to, and didn't actually understand why she thought she should. Instead, she reached out her hand, curling her fingers into the hair of the man running the tip of his tongue along the inside of her thigh. She draped her other arm back, around the man behind her, mirroring her own action as she sank her hand into his hair.

There was a sweet, throbbing pulse coursing through her, she felt it pushing her to tense between them, to let her muscles go taut as they went on, kissing and stroking her.

It was as she cried out, the blissful warmth nearly too much for her to bear, that she felt twin stings. Quick, sharp searing at her throat, at that soft, sensitive, inner-most place on her right thigh. The pleasure dancing through her made focusing on the pain impossible—or perhaps the pain even added to it.

As it ebbed, she collapsed back against the man behind her. She thought she must be drifting to sleep once more as he folded his arms around her in a possessive embrace while the one before her lifted his head.

He kissed her once more as her eyelids drooped.

She had no idea which one of them spoke, but she felt certain she heard the words, "I told you she was the one meant for us."

∞∞∞

Violet awoke the next morning to bright sunshine washing through that window over the desk. She pulled herself to sit up, her thoughts a bit tangled and hazy.

She was quite certain she'd dreamed something *rather* vivid, but could not recall just now what that might've been.

Climbing out of bed to gather her things so

she might wash up and dress, she winced. She felt rested, but also sore .... Perhaps she'd slept funny.

Putting the matter out of her mind, she prepared for her day. Or, rather, prepared to locate the master of the house and her prospective student, and deliver them her answer.

∞∞∞

She found them in the dining room, though she'd tried not to get overwhelmed by the sheer size and grandeur of the estate as she bumbled her way around. At the wide open double doors, she halted, noting that a place had been set for her at the table.

"Good—good morning," she said, forcing a smile.

Ives grinned at the sound of her voice, turning warm blue eyes on her. "I hope you slept well. Please don't think us forward in having a place set for you. We had no way of knowing your decision, and it would be quite rude to send you off without offering you a meal after the night you had, regardless."

For a moment, Violet was transfixed by his gaze. Shaking her head, she focused on his words. "That's actually quite thoughtful, thank you, but ...." She nervously darted her tongue out to wet her lips. Cassius had not looked up when she came in; indeed, he appeared rather grumpily fixated on his plate.

Clearing her throat, she started, again. "But I've decided to accept the post."

Ives' grin broadened, and Cassius snapped up his gaze to lock on her. Astonishment shone in his face. "You...?"

Nodding, she smiled again. She also ignored that those blue eyes set off the strangest winging of warm, giddy butterflies through her stomach. She was feeling *giddy* far too often in regard to this place and its residents. Her decision had *nothing* to do with the attractiveness of either of her employers, just as it had nothing to do with her perfect and pretty room.

He required her aid, and she'd never had it in her to refuse those so genuinely in need. If she could improve his life, how could she possibly say no?

Answering his question from last night, she said, "I *am* going to help you."

She ignored another flash—this one of lips against her skin and fingers slipping beneath her clothes, how odd, odd and flustering, and she put the sensation out of her head immediately—as a relieved smile broke across Cassius Vaughn's face. It was the first time she'd seen a happy expression on him since meeting him yesterday evening.

And she was just a little afraid of the way her heart skipped a beat at the sight.

Chapter Five

Vulnerabilities

*D*earest Fletcher,

  I do believe these letters of yours are the most you have ever written in your life. I know this is hardly ideal and you're accustomed to me being so close, but I assure you, I am well. Yes, the house is a bit . . . larger than I am accustomed to from previous employers' homes, and it is a little lonesome here. It's very dark at night in the country, which can sometimes lend to imaginations running amok, I suppose. Rest assured, I am having no such problems.

  You needn't worry about me so. I will remind you

that you have your own work to see to, and a wedding to look forward to in the coming months. I'm certain if you find yourself lacking for activities, Grace kind find any number of tasks to occupy your time.

Yours sincerely,
Violet

She read over her letter, a whimsical smile lighting her features. Violet truly never had seen the young man sit down to write as often as he had since she'd arrived at Winterbury Hall. The first letter arrived shortly after she'd written home to inform them that she'd accepted the position. She'd expected him to write, certainly, but not so quickly.

Of course, she'd not mentioned the strangeness of the solitary and quiet Gilbert—who somehow managed to successfully fulfill the roles of bulter, cook, footman, *any* position Lord Hayward required at any moment, in fact, with seemingly little effort or wear—nor that she was having odd dreams in her letters. Fletcher would only fuss, and being so very far from her, he'd fuss even more and simply drive Grace and Uncle Hugh spare.

No, she insisted to herself, folding the letter carefully. She only needed a little more time to adjust to the isolation of the country.

She wanted everything about this post to be splendid, and therefore it was her responsibility to make that a reality.

∞∞∞

With an aggravated sigh, Cassius swiped a hand across the table, sending the collection of skillfully placed utensils to the floor.

Violet cringed at the sharp, clattering sound of metal against the marble tiles. Inhaling deep through her nostrils, she exhaled slow as she pressed her fingertips to her temples.

Nearly three weeks had passed at her new post, and it seemed only a few hours into each morning—before they were even served lunch, in fact—her *student* would decide it the ideal time to throw a tantrum. She could only assume that despite his request for her assistance, he was so accustomed to his tutors acquiescing to his whims that having a proper fit when he found himself frustrated by his lessons usually saw to the end of said lessons.

She carefully schooled her features as she knelt to retrieve the silverware. "Cassius, I understand this may *seem* ridiculous, but proper etiquette dictates that one must—"

"Proper etiquette dictates that one must use a different fork for each course of a meal, ignoring that they all serve *exactly* the same purpose?" He frowned as he watched her reach around him to replace the utensils with delicate fingers and careful movements.

"I know it's a bit absurd," she said, offering a smile that was both gracious and understanding, "but, as you will learn, proper etiquette calls for a great many things that *are* rather absurd."

"And so I'm expected to patiently accept this . . . *absurdity*?" He frowned, shaking his head. "Why?"

Violet was sadly aware there was no true, satisfactory answer for such a question. Etiquette was pure nonsense—a salad tasted no different if eaten with a dinner fork, pudding no less rich if consumed from a soup spoon—but it *was* how society functioned. "Because *everyone* does. That's what makes learning it important."

She bit back a yawn. Not only were Cassius' antics wearing, but she felt certain each night thus far, she'd had another of those terribly inappropriate dreams she couldn't quite recall— thank Heaven for small favors—which had inevitably caused her to spend half the night tossing and turning.

He sighed, dragging his hands down his face, and then turned his gaze toward the nearest window. "It just feels *so* bloody pointless."

Her shoulders sloped a bit at his tone. Unlike the previous lessons, he didn't sound agitated, he sounded . . . *resigned*. She suddenly wondered just how fast it was that her predecessors had abandoned their post.

Changing tactics, she lowered herself once more to kneel beside his chair. "I understand the simplest things can prove the most difficult to retain, but etiquette *is* part of your education."

His blue eyes flicked down to meet hers for the briefest second before he returned his attention to the sun-brightened window. "Perhaps if we could move onto another lesson and come back to this?"

Violet tipped her head to one side as she thought about which of his lessons Cassius might take to with the most ease. Clearly anything that required too much effort on his part was something they would have to work their way up to.

In that moment, she noticed how his gaze was fastened to that window and the bright world beyond its glass panes. He seemed fascinated by it . . . but then, she supposed that made sense. After all, from what Ives had told her of Cassius' upbringing, he probably hadn't spent very much time outside the estate's walls.

My, she thought, studying him as he studied the window, *he certainly is a handsome one.*

Why did it seem every time she let herself think on how attractive he was, there was some fleeting image in the back of her mind? Those pretty hands sliding along her bare thighs . . . his perfect lips ghosting over her skin . . . .

The sensation of warmth flooding her cheeks startled her. Giving herself a shake, Violet stood up before he could notice.

Her sudden movement drew his gaze and she found him staring at her again.

"So, may we?"

Furrowing her brow, she only looked back at him in confusion for a moment. "What? Oh!" Shaking her head, she uttered a quiet laugh at herself. "Move onto a different lesson. Certainly! Though, I believe I've an idea on that. If you'll excuse me a moment?" In her scramble to answer him, a notion *had* occurred to her.

She turned and took a step before Cassius' hand latching around her wrist caused her to halt in place. The touch of his skin against hers was cool, as always; she imagined that was some residual effect of being ill for so long.

The reminder made it difficult for her not to reach out and place her free hand over his as she pivoted back to face him. She'd made that mistake on her second day and it seemed such comforting gestures only caused him to recoil into himself.

"What is it?"

His brows drew together, making for a painfully lost expression that lasted only the briefest second before it was gone again. "Where are you going?"

She wondered if she had imagined that wounded look. "I'm going to ask Ives something. As I said, I've an idea, but it would require his approval."

Holding her gaze, Cassius nodded and let his fingers slip from her wrist.

Nodding back, she turned again, crossing the room. As she stepped through the door, however, she once more thought she must be imagining things.

Cassius' whispered assessment that Ives would agree to *any* suggestion that might fall from her lips could only be flight of whimsy all her own.

As she lifted her hand to knock on the door of Ives' study—well, his *favorite* study, as there were already three of which Violet was aware, and she'd only explored a meager portion of the estate, thus far—she felt the oddest prickling on the back of her neck. There was the faintest rush of air against her ear.

Frowning, she backpedaled half a step, her gaze sweeping the length of the third-floor wing lay in the opposite direction.

The stretch of doors further along was dark, deeply shadowed by heavy curtains drawn over the windows. Yet, in the center of the corridor . . . .

Swallowing hard, her eyes narrowed as she focused. The air caught in her throat, though she hardly noticed, distracted by the odd silhouette—the lone figure, darker and thicker than the other shadows surrounding it.

Squeezing her eyes closed, she forced herself to breathe as she knocked.

"Enter."

At the sound of Ives' deep, melodic voice, she opened her eyes. The silhouette had vanished.

Inhaling deep through her nostrils, she squared her shoulders and gave her head a shake. Clearly her assessment from a few minutes ago had been correct. Her overwrought state *was* causing her imagination to run away with her.

Well, then the fresh air provided by her idea would probably do *her* some good as well as Cassius.

Opening the door, she poked her head inside. Of course, Ives appeared magnificent in his perfectly ordered suit as he looked over some papers spread out before him on his desk.

"I'm sorry to interrupt, Ives. Do you have a moment?"

His head came up instantly, the delicate skin beneath his blue eyes crinkling as he smiled at her. "For *you*, Violet? Always."

Clearing her throat quietly, she pretended her heart didn't flutter a little at his words. He was only being kind, after all. She should be accustomed to his consistently polite manner by now, she thought. No need to read too much into pleasantries.

Smiling in response, she stepped inside. Shutting the door, she clasped her hands behind her as she crossed the room to stand before his desk.

"Don't you look like a spot of sunlight in the

morning?"

She bit the inside of her lip to keep her expression from brightening any further. Though, she liked to think his comment meant he fancied her dress—lemon-yellow, with the simple pattern of delicate, windswept white flower petals.

"Thank you. I need to speak to you about Cassius."

Dark brows shooting up, he glanced at the grandfather clock on the side of the room. "So soon?" he asked, running his hand through his hair. "Here I'd thought he was getting better."

Following his gaze, Violet glanced at the clock, as well. "Oh, no, no," she said with a breezy laugh.

Each day they discussed how lessons were proceeding over afternoon tea. Cassius usually saw fit to stare off and do his level-best to appear listless, his arms folded across his chest, like a bored child pretending he could not overhear his parents discussing his punishment for misbehavior.

"I was actually wondering if I may be . . . permitted to take Cassius off the estate's grounds."

A serious expression tugging at his handsome features, Ives sat forward in his seat. Propping his elbows on his desk, he clasped his hands in front of his mouth.

Violet's face fell immediately, fearing she'd overstepped her bounds.

"Cassius," he began, his voice grave, "has not

been outside these walls in some time. His vulnerability due to his past circumstances makes me cautious, as I'm certain you can understand. Why do you ask for this?"

Shrugging, she dropped her gaze to the front panel of his finely polished cherrywood desk. "Cassius is frustrated by his etiquette lessons, probably because of the monotony. He asked that we move onto a different subject, so I thought . . . ." She darted out her tongue, moistening her lips—though her diverted attention kept her from noticing that Ives was not oblivious to the nervous gesture. "I thought perhaps I could take him to a museum? If I were to move onto anything to put off a frustrating lesson, it would be art anyway, as he seems to enjoy that most. That aside, getting out of the house for a few hours *might* be good for him."

When she met Ives' eyes once more, some of the severity had drained from his expression. His eyebrows were drawn up ever so slightly in surprise.

Elated suddenly that she had his interest, she offered a slip of a grin. "Maybe if he can be there, *amongst* the art, immersed in it, it might be the spark he needs. You were correct, Cassius is *quite* intelligent; every day I see it—intelligent enough to argue the necessity of a great many of the subjects you mean for me to teach him—but he simply doesn't absorb anything. We can't keep waiting and hoping he'll change in this. I believe this is where, and how, his previous tutors failed him. I think the problem is that standard lessons simply don't engage him."

"So a more involved, hands-on approach is what you're suggesting?"

She nodded. "It certainly couldn't do any harm."

∞∞∞

The look of shock on Cassius' face was more immensely rewarding to Violet than she'd predicted it would be as they stepped from the carriage. His blue eyes were wide and his mouth had dropped open a bit as he stared up at the museum's domed edifice.

They'd departed the estate grounds after lunch, Ives insisting that they eat before they spend hours outside the house. Given Cassius' history, Violet had agreed the delay was probably best.

In the rays of afternoon sunlight, the faint dusting of color his cheeks usually held seemed to vanish. As she reached up to touch his face, she found his skin felt slightly chilled even through the fabric of her gloves. She worried that the lengthy carriage ride had proved too much exertion for him, already.

He started at the press of her fingers on his jaw, but didn't shy away from the gesture. Instead, he merely dropped his gaze to meet hers.

"Are you feeling all right?" she asked, nodding back toward the carriage. "If you can't manage this, we can go back, and maybe another day —"

"No, no." Cassius clasped one of his gloved hands around hers and gently pulled her fingers from his face. "I suspect that given my lack of exposure to the elements, I'm simply more vulnerable to the coolness of the air than one might expect."

There was that word again, *vulnerable*; she only hoped such excursions would help to strengthen him rather than harm him. "If you're certain . . . ." She tried not to think too much on how he'd yet to release her hand.

"I am. Why didn't you tell me you were taking me to a museum?"

Violet couldn't help a grin, then. "Surprise."

∞∞∞∞

"Now," he said, seeming a little shocked as she looped her arm around his elbow, yet he didn't pull away, "would I be correct in guessing this is some new, mad idea of yours for an art lesson?"

"Yes and no," she answered as they strolled past gorgeous antique sculptures and paintings that touched on the breathtaking realism of the Renaissance period. "For today, we're only looking."

Nodding, a thoughtful frown tugged at the corners of his mouth as he glanced around.

"*Today* you're simply going to find which ones strike your interest most." She inhaled deep and let the breath out, slow and measured. "On our *next* trip here, you'll learn about those specific works."

"We're to do this again?"

Violet pursed her lips, holding in a laugh at the exhilaration in his voice. "Yes. We can make this a weekly outing, if you like. And, of course, *if* you're feeling up to it."

The grin lighting her features at his response was not lost on him. "What's the look for?"

She shrugged. "I'm simply happy to see you excited about one of your lessons. Makes me think perhaps we should do something *really* daring . . . like having your etiquette lessons at a café!"

Cassius pulled her to a halt, his surprised look giving way to a feigned scowl. "You're making fun of me."

She felt a little, giddy stirring in the pit of her stomach, but told herself it was on account of how well her idea had played out. Nothing to do with their flirting . . . because they *weren't* flirting.

That would be highly inappropriate.

"Well," she said, smiling once more, "perhaps if you stop fussing over silly things, I'll stop treating you as though *you're* the thing that's silly."

Biting his lip, he nodded. Though she couldn't help but notice that his eyes narrowed as they moved over her in a quick, but appraising sweep before he turned and started them walking, once more.

For a time, they wandered the floors and exhibits in shifting bouts of comfortable silence and lighthearted chatting. She kept a mental note of which pieces seemed to capture his attention longer than the others.

She noticed how dark it was getting as they had almost completed rounding the top floor. The diminished light was not only a result not of the sun through the windows sinking low in the sky, but also that a portion of this level had been curtained off.

"Why is this area closed?"

Shaking her head, she glanced about. "Repairs, or possibly prepartion for a new exhibit being installed?"

At this, Cassius began thinking aloud over the possibilites of what said new exhibits might be. But Violet didn't quite hear him. She found her gaze trapped by the nearby sculptures. Not in artistic favor currently, but beautiful nonetheless. Greco-Roman style depictions of godlike figures and lovers in passionate embraces dominated the space, here.

The statues cast shadows against the walls that were somehow warped yet graceful, and for a moment, she imagined . . . .

The press of a body against hers . . . . The sweet tingling rush of a mouth at her throat, of lips skimming the delicate skin of her inner thigh as hands cupped her breasts and gentle fingers parted—

She tore her gaze from those elegantly twisted shadows and forced a breath, willing her cheeks to stay cool and her pulse not to race.

After a few heartbeats, she managed to calm herself enough to return her attention to Cassius. Yet, as she lifted her eyes to his, she found him already watching her face.

His brows drawing upward, he asked in a low voice, "Saw something you fancy, did you?"

Swallowing hard, she gave herself a shake. Clearly, he only meant to ask if she liked the sculptures—there was *no* way he could know what had just flashed past her mind's eye.

"Actually, I noticed it's getting late," she said, forcing a small smile onto her lips. "We should really return to Winterbury, now."

Despite what she thought was likely disappointment flicking across his features, Cassius nodded and turned them back toward the staircase.

Chapter Six

Shadows

Cassius retired to his room directly when they arrived home. Not that Violet could very much blame him, she could barely recall having been ill a day in her life, yet *she* was tired.

Ives was nowhere to be found. She considereed that perhaps he was in his study, again, as she climbed the stairs to the second-floor. The night-darkened corridors, sparsely illuminated by intermittent lanterns, called to mind the image she'd seen earlier that day.

Sighing, she lifted her gaze to the third-floor landing... and stopped cold.

There was that silhouette, again. Darker and thicker than the surrounding shadows, just like before, but now it appeared to lean over the upper railing....

As though it were peering down at her.

A shiver danced up her spine as she stared back at it. "Wha—?" As the whispered syllable fell from her lips, the thing pulled back, vanishing into the blackness of the floor above.

In the silhouette's sudden absence, Violet felt strangely emboldened. She didn't like being frightened. Even less did she like being frightened in a place she was meant to call home, no matter how temporarily.

"Oh, *no* you don't," she said, her voice slipping out in an angry tumble of words. Snatching the lantern from the end table nearest the second-floor landing, she gathered her skirts in her free hand and hurried up the steps to the level above.

The massive house was quiet as she climbed; she could hear the creak of the boards beneath her feet despite the plush carpet that ran the length of the staircase. Everything was so very still, she thought she could feel the weight of the air, itself, pressing down on her.

As she stepped out onto the third-floor landing, she drew a deep breath and let it out slow before she turned toward the long end of the corridor.

A wisp of inky blackness flickered against the shadows.

Despite the sensation of ice pooling in the pit of her stomach, Violet squared her shoulders and lifted her chin. This was a matter of her imagination running away with her, *again*.

She started down the corridor, toward the wing where she'd seen this afternoon's looming silhouette. She *had* to prove to herself it was nothing—some trick of the shadows on her tired mind, *nothing* more!

When she reached the place where that shape had stood earlier, the fine hairs stood on the back of her neck . . . . Just as they had when she'd seen the thing, but now gooseflesh prickled her skin, beneath the sleeve of her dress.

But only one on side of her body.

Glancing down her left sleeve, she continued lower with her gaze, along the floor, and then up to a door. Unlike the others, it was open, by a hair's breadth; not enough to be noticeable from further down the corridor . . . . *Nor* enough to let a breeze pass through.

With a determined frown, she pivoted to face the door directly. Darting her gaze up and down the length of the wing once more, she stepped forward and gripped the knob.

Violet winced at the whining and creaking that met her ears as she pushed open the door. Shaking off the unnerved feeling left in the wake of that sound, she stepped into the room, lifting the lantern to look about.

Cobwebs wreathed every item and corner, whirls of dust hung in the air within the sphere of illumination cast by the light in her hand. The standing metal cabinets and glass-doored cupboard, the leather chaise and stiff, narrow bed made her think . . . .

This was—or had been—a doctor's examination room.

She forced a gulp as her attention tripped along the desk in the corner and its accompanying black-cushioned chair. It made sense that there was such a room within the estate, given Cassius' past, she supposed, but . . . .

This place seemed out of use *far* too long to have been utilized as recently as only a few years ago.

Something shot through the darkness, and Violet turned toward it, her free hand rummaging behind her. As her gaze searched the room for whatever had moved, she groped blindly, hoping to find something she could use to defend herself.

Cold, hard fingers scraped against her own. Before she could stop herself, a scream tore from her throat and she ran for the door.

She collided with something immediately in the corridor, but held back her voice this time. A hand steadied hers, keeping her from dropping the lantern.

"My goodness, you're white as a sheet!"

Violet heard Ives' voice, deep and soothing

in her ear, as his other arm wrapped around her shoulders.

"Violet, darling, you're shivering," he whispered, holding her against his chest. "I thought I'd heard something this way. Who would've thought it would be you? Whatever are you doing over here?"

She drew a shaking breath before she could respond. "I—I saw something, I wanted it to be my imagination so ... I followed it ...."

By the tone of his voice, she could tell his brows had shot up and he was smiling as he said, "You're a very brave girl, then ... or a very stupid one."

"Feeling a bit of both just now, thanks."

He nodded but held back a laugh, feeling her shivers subside, and leaned back to catch her gaze. "Let's go have a look, then, shall we?"

Ives slipped his free hand over one of hers, and stepped around her to step through the door.

"Something touched my hand," she said, so close behind him her voice was nearly muffled by his shoulder. "I was reaching back and something touched my hand."

From her vantage point, she could not see the smile curving his mouth. "Well, then here." Pausing for only a moment, he turned, still holding her hand.

Violet tried not to breathe too deep as the movement put his face right over hers due to how close they stood. He pressed the lantern into her free hand.

"There," he said, holding her gaze. "Now both your hands are occupied. That will keep you from grabbing for anything in the dark."

She nodded and then he turned away, leading her back into the room.

"When my father was young, there was an in-house doctor." He tugged her up to stand beside him and slipped his fingers over the hand which held the lantern. "This old house is so far from everything that such an arrangement proved most convenient."

Ives directed Violet's hand, moving the lantern's light to sweep the room. "Of course, the place was all but forgotten about when it came time to help Cassius. The rooms down this corridor ... I sometimes forget about them, *altogether.* Father stopped using this wing when my mother passed, so I never used it, either."

"Perhaps you should examine these rooms, put them to use again," she said, her words soft and thoughtful.

"That's a notion." He sighed, quite apparently not thinking when he relinquished his hold on her empty hand to rest his arm around her shoulders. "I suppose I never considered it. One day, Father caught me playing in here—I think I'd never actually been in this room before that day —and punished me so harshly, I decided I would never come here, again."

"Oh." Her brow furrowed as she risked a

glance at his face. Lord Ives Hayward looked posi-tively lost in his memories. "I'm sorry, I didn't real-ize."

"How could you?" he asked, a gentle smile curving his lips. "But you are right. Perhaps it would do me some good to let go of the past. Any-way . . . . Whatever had frightened you, do you see it now?"

Violet stepped forward, out from beneath the protective weight of his arm and scanned the room. The black thing that had shot across the floor was nowhere to be seen.

But whatever had touched her hand had been *behind* her.

She pivoted in a slow movement, adjusting the height of the lantern—Ives' hand still over hers—to see clearly behind him. Dust clung to the once-white bones, hanging limp from the metal stand behind them.

Her entire frame slumped as she huffed out a sigh of relief. Ives seemed to notice the change in her posture and again circled her shoulders with his arm, steadying her.

"It was only a physician's skeleton. Oh, I feel *so* silly! I should have realized."

"Not at all. Generally, no one has reason to expect that a skeleton standing behind them is a *normal* thing."

He was poking fun at her, she knew, but she couldn't help a laugh in spite of herself. "I suppose you're right. Still." She shook her head, upset with herself for behaving in such a ridiculous manner. "I am so sorry I made such a fuss. I haven't been sleeping well, and I suppose it's caught up with me."

"Ah, I understand." He began guiding her toward the door. "Well, then, let's get you to your room. It's a bit early for bed, but I think the extra time to rest might do you some good."

Violet found herself suddenly fighting back a yawn as they left the deserted wing behind and started down the stairs for the second-floor. "I'm not sure a few extra hours will make a difference. I've been having, um—" She cut herself off, nervously licking her lips. Ives still had his arm around her, and it was difficult not to wonder what those dreams she couldn't quite recall might be about with him so close. "*Odd* dreams. They've been causing me trouble sleeping."

He nodded, but fell quiet until they reached her room. Finally, he released her and pushed open the door for her.

Handing the lantern off to him, Violet stepped across the threshold. Just as quickly, she was stopped by Ives' fingers circling her wrist.

Startled, she looked back at him.

He smiled warmly. "Just rest, Violet. I promise you, no dreams will visit you tonight. I'll have Gilbert set a tray beside your door, in case you rouse later and would like dinner."

She nodded, smiling back. "Thank you, Ives." And then the door was closed between

61

them.

Letting out a noisy yawn only after she heard his retreating footfalls reach the end of the corridor, she gave a stretch and began undressing.

Somewhere between removing her stockings and slipping on her nightdress, she recalled the sound of Ives' voice as he'd tried to calm her. *Violet,* darling, *you're shivering.*

Ives had called her darling . . . during a moment of duress. During the sort of moment when people didn't guard the things that fell from their lips.

She sat on the edge of her bed somewhat limply. Lord Ives Hayward, II had called *her* darling.

Oh, how was she supposed to sleep *now* with these ghastly, damnable *giddy* butterflies zipping about in her stomach?

Chapter Seven

What the Heart Wants

Violet,

I know you won't believe me, but life has become rather dull in your absence. Please, do make sure you write to Grace soon—she's driving the rest of us mad. And Uncle, as well. . . . He was relieved to learn that you're adjusting well to life at Winterbury, I think. He seems rather unhappy to have you so far from the family.

Also, don't tell her I said so, but I think Grace is worried that you're enjoying country life so much that you'll forget your promise to be her Maid of Honor.

We all miss you terribly. Write back soon.

Keep safe,
Fletcher

Violet snickered at that—as though she could ever forget such a thing? She'd received Fletcher's most recent letter a few days ago, but was only getting to it just this morning. She was admittedly a bit ashamed that she'd not made reading it more of a priority.

He always ended his letters in the same manner. Asking her to write back soon, closing by telling her to *keep safe*.

She shook her head as she took up her pen. Honestly. What could he possibly think posed her a danger—

A sudden crash of splintering glass made her jump. Setting the missive and her pen aside, she stood from her writing desk and hurried to the door.

Muffled voices met her ears, rushed and angry, as she eased open the door and peered out. From her room, she could see clear down the corridor, into the other wing, where Cassius and Ives' bedrooms were.

Yet another week had passed since their trip to the museum. Her sleep had been *mostly* dreamless in that time—though, she felt certain that on at least two mornings, she had awoken from another of those terribly inappropriate ones —and Cassius had been *mostly* cooperative in his studies.

Perhaps hoping for that trend to last was too much to ask for, she considered as she watched Ives pleading with a rather disgruntled-looking Cassius just in front of Cassius' open bedroom door.

The younger man was gesturing wildly, his perfect mouth turned downward in an expression of *severe* displeasure. Ives had his hands in the air, his tone low, obviously controlled, giving him the appearance of someone trying to talk down a raging animal.

Then, everything seemed to still around her as Cassius turned his head, those blue eyes locking on hers. She couldn't help the start she gave as she stared back at him.

As he held her attention rapt, she could not stop the untoward image that skittered through her mind. It must be something she'd dreamed, because the impression of Cassius standing so very close to her that he was pressing her body flush against a wall behind her with his own was not based in anything that had *actually* happened. That his lips had closed over hers in hungry but teasing nibbles that just now caused a blush in her cheeks and a tingling warmth to zip through her, was a memory with *no* basis in reality.

Of course, that had to have been a dream, because no such thing had—or *could* have—happened! Perhaps it was the effect of such seclusion on one's sanity, just as Ives had warned her.

But then Ives looked over, as well. Dear Lord, she hoped that telltale blush caused by those thoughts she should *not* be having had faded from her cheeks!

Ives heaved a sigh, pivoting on his heel to stride through the corridor toward her.

Behind him, Cassius tore his gaze from Violet's, shaking his head as he raked a hand through the waves of his unusually disheveled brown hair. She was so acutely aware of everything he did, even as she shifted her attention to Ives.

Ives' face, already closer than she'd expected, was a sweet shock to her system, all its own. As though she constantly forgot how staggeringly handsome he was whenever she wasn't looking directly at him.

She bit her lip to hold in a frown. If she could not get these feelings of hers under control, she might have to resign her post.

The disappointment at even considering leaving them seemed in danger of breaking her heart.

As Ives finally reached her, she forced a smile. "Is everything all right?"

Wincing, he glanced briefly over his shoulder at her student. "I think perhaps, today, he may need a break from his lessons. He's feeling a bit ... more temperamental than usual."

Violet's shoulders drooped. "Well, if you believe that's best."

"Although, if you don't mind an extra task, then I have something that might occupy your time when you are not overseeing his studies?"

"Oh?" Her brows shot up.

Slipping an arm around her, he turned her and started guiding her along the corridor toward the staircase. Though she kept her gaze on the floor, she was still acutely aware of Cassius watching them from his open bedroom door.

Unable to stop herself, she darted her attention from the beautiful pattern of the carpet beneath her feet, up and over her shoulder to Cassius' face, but only for half a heartbeat. Just long enough to glimpse his expression.

He no longer looked as angry as he had a moment ago when he'd been carrying on whatever whispered argument that was with Ives. He looked sad, now. She could never quite understand how it was that he managed to remind her of a lost child and an old man weary with the world around him, all at once.

Again she bit her lip, this time at the sensation of the bitter unhappiness in those blue eyes tearing at her heart.

"You recall your . . . little adventure in the doctor's office, last week?"

Clearing her throat, Violet focused on Ives. She forced an airy little laugh. "Vividly."

"And you recall suggesting I revisit the rooms in that wing? Put them to use, again?"

"I do."

As they reached the landing, he turned her again, this time to face him. "I will understand if you say no, as this is not at all what you hired on for, but ... I would like for *you* to go through those rooms."

She furrowed her brow, uncertain what to think of his request. "Me?"

His broad shoulders drooped a little at the surprise in her tone. He didn't want her to think he expected her to serve as a maid, as well, so he hurried on. "I thought you might familiarize yourself with that wing, and perhaps ... help me decide what's to be done with those rooms."

Violet was uncertain again, her eyes shooting wide. This was certainly not the first time he exhibited a willingness to take her opinion about his home into account. Only a few days ago, she'd commented offhandedly that some flowers in the foyer and parlor would brighten the feel of the house. The very next morning, she'd come downstairs to find a lovely array of blossoms from the garden in both places.

She was touched that he continually tried to make her feel welcome—to think of Winterbury Hall as somewhere she belonged and not merely her place of employment.

It did give her pause, however, as it made her wonder just how long he expected her to stay on here. More troublingly, it made her aware that part of her hoped that the answer to that question

—if she ever dared ask it—would be *forever*.

As though reading her thoughts, he smiled gently. "I want you to feel this is your home. So . . . if, for example, you should ever decide you wish to use that wing for yourself, that is what we will do."

Somehow, her eyes grew wider, still. "Are you quite serious?"

Ives let out a surprised laugh. "I didn't realize I was so prone to joking that you would believe I'm not."

"Oh, well, um, I . . . ." Frowning thoughtfully, she nodded. More than just the idea of him *giving* her a wing of the house—*if* she chose to use it for herself—but her curiosity about those rooms was suddenly a rabid thing, indeed. He'd told her those rooms had not been in use since he was a child. She couldn't help imagining what they might contain.

"All right, yes. I accept the task."

Several hours must've passed easily, she thought, as she sat back on her heels and wiped the back of her wrist across her brow. She'd headed to the unused wing of the third-floor nearly the moment she'd finished breakfast. While Ives had told her the rooms he thought the wing contained—a study, a small library, possibly a guest suite, or two, and, of course, that doctor's office—she was more than aware of Cassius' attention on her.

She'd turned to look at him, finding that rather than eating, he was merely pushing his food around his plate with his fork.

With a sigh, she'd reached out, moving slow so he had the opportunity to pull out of her grasp. Even with all the progress they'd made, and how much more comfortable he seemed in her presence now than he had those first few days, she always treated him gingerly, in case he might decide himself *un*comfortable around her, again.

But he didn't pull away as she rested her hand over his. Rather, he dropped his gaze to her fingers, as though the gesture puzzled him.

"You really should eat, Cassius," she said, her tone thoughtful.

She tried to keep her features schooled as he answered her touch by rubbing the pad of his thumb across her knuckles in a delicate sweep. Such a simple thing, and yet it set off a tingling warmth within her.

Violet chanced a glance at Ives, trying to gauge his reaction to this. He seemed to merely observe the interaction, as though this display of affection—even small and simple as it was—were perfectly normal.

Swallowing hard, Cassius chewed at his bottom lip a moment before he spoke. "I'm sorry."

She was taken aback by those two words. "For what?"

"I wanted to go the museum again, today. You said we could go every week *if* I was feeling up to it, and I'm simply not today and I'm sorry."

He sounded so upset, but the way in which he was speaking, she realized he was upset with *himself*.

Her brow furrowed as she shook her head. "That's what you were so angry about earlier?"

"Seems rather ridiculous when you state is so plainly," he said, shrugging. "But yes. I thought you might be disappointed."

A sad little smile curving her lips, she tightened her grip on his hand. "Oh, no. I mean, yes, I did very much enjoy seeing you take to the idea of having your art lessons there, but I'm not disappointed. Your health is far more important. The museum will still be there when you're feeling better."

"You treat me far too kindly." He mirrored her expression, his blue eyes narrowing so that delicate lines creased his skin at the corners. "Why did we only find you *now*?"

Violet's brows shot up as her smile melted. Did he think those other tutors had wasted their time on him that greatly?

"Fate works in mysterious ways," Ives said, his voice faraway. His gaze was on the window across the room as he took a leisurely sip of his breakfast tea.

She kept her focus on Cassius. "While I'm working in the unused wing today, I would like you to do something for me."

His smile reflected in his eyes then, and she realized how very much that little change affected his entire appearance. The weary old man she swore she glimpsed in him sometimes was gone in that moment. "Anything."

"Spend today in the gardens." When his only response was to arch his brow, she uttered an airy giggle and went on. "Fresh air, sunlight. I want you to relax, but I don't want it to be in this old, stuffy house."

Ives scoffed. "My home is *not* stuffy!"

Violet and Cassius looked to the other man, then. Though his gaze was still on the window, a ghost of a smirk plucked one corner of his mouth upward.

They all shared a quick laugh at his feigned indignation.

Then, in a flash, Violet remembered her hand still over Cassius'. Remembered the gentle stroking of his thumb across her skin . . . which he had been carrying on this entire time.

Returning her attention to their joined hands, she felt her face fall and a flare of warmth in her cheeks. *Why?* He'd been doing this for minutes, now, but suddenly something had shifted.

Forcing a gulp down her throat, she brought her gaze up to his. His expression was also serious, now. The change made her aware that he'd sensed that shift, as well.

Clearing her throat, she slipped her hand from his and scooted back her chair from the table. "I suppose I had better get to work, then."

As she turned away and crossed the room, she was certain she could feel both men watching her. The moment she was out the double doors, she pressed her back to one and drew a deep, steadying breath.

She was certain, now. She couldn't leave them, but did she have much choice if she couldn't stop these inappropriate feelings?

They were her *employers* . . . they'd probably be mortified if they knew of her growing affection for them! They probably had no idea what their touches and looks were doing to her.

"It's happening, isn't it?" Violet started at Ives' voice, but luckily the motion was not enough to jar the door against which she leaned.

"What?"

He snickered at Cassius' mystified tone. *"You are falling in love with her."* It wasn't a question.

She clamped a hand over her mouth to hold in a shocked gasp at the accusation.

She expected a denial—she braced herself for a scoffing brush off. Her feelings might be inappropriate, but his objection would still hurt.

"As are you. Don't think I haven't noticed."

Violet dropped her hand, pressing it over her heart. No, no. This wasn't possible. Not only was Cassius *not* denying it, he was accusing Ives of the very same thing?

There was a forlorn sigh—from Ives, probably. *"Well . . . best we keep our feelings in check, then. Don't want to frighten the poor girl away with such . . . improper inclinations."*

She reminded herself to breathe. Not only did they feel as she did, but they felt the same way about the situation?

Violet willed herself to calm down. If they viewed the situation as she did, then that was good. Nothing could come of these feelings if they all recognized that such emotions could not be entertained.

Drawing in a deep breath, she nodded to herself and finally peeled away from the doors.

∞∞∞

At the sound of her footfalls drifting away from the door—they could tell from the way she moved that she thought she was being quiet—Ives flicked his gaze toward the entryway and grinned.

"All in order," he said, lifting his tea for another lazy sip.

Cassius propped his elbow on the table and braced his chin against the heel of his palm. "I wonder if she knows *how* important her feelings are in all this."

Ives offered the other man a wink. "As long as we're being genuine, she'll come around if she's not there, already. After all, she only heard the truth."

Chapter Eight

A Lovely View

She knew she'd ignored Gilbert's words as he'd poked his head into the study and informed her it was lunchtime. After overhearing Cassius and Ives speak on their feelings, she wasn't certain she was ready to sit for a meal with them, again.

Perhaps at tea.

There were so many interesting things in this room. Books bearing titles she'd never heard of, old family journals she was simply itching to sit and read through, aged portraits. She could see Ives' resemblance to his father, Lord Ives Hayward, I, and his father before him. She did wonder, though she'd never dare ask, if the family had fallen upon hardtimes once, as some images portrayed fine gentlemen clad in outdated attire, if she were judging the passing of years correctly.

But the place certainly *was* dusty—she would not be surprised if there were little tufts of grey clinging to the mussed strands that had fallen from her pinned-up hair.

Climbing to her feet, she wiped her filthy hands on the borrowed apron she'd tied 'round her waist. Now that she'd paused, she was starting to feel hungry. Oh, well, she'd have a good appetite for dinner, she supposed. Or shamelessly devour the entire tray of biscuits at tea by herself.

She made her way to the window, breathing deep of the fresh air breezing through. With a sad little laugh at herself, she shook her head.

Honestly, the moment she overhead their words she should've gone right back into the dining room and resigned her post. Her own feelings she could have continued ignoring, but she shouldn't be here. Not now that she knew they harbored similar emotions toward her.

No matter how she might justify her decision to stay, this was a breeding ground for scandal!

She sighed, a small, sad sound, and closed her eyes. She didn't *actually* care about any of that, did she? She *wanted* to be here, even knowing what folly it could be.

When had she become so very disinterested in propriety? Well . . . when she came to think of Winterbury Hall as home, more than likely.

Opening her eyes again, she looked out into the gardens. There was Cassius, just as he'd promised.

Sitting on the lip of one of the grey stone fountains that dotted the property, he had a book open in his lap. He seemed completely absorbed in his literature.

There it was. The reason she couldn't leave. That fluttering sensation in her chest as she observed him simply sitting out there, reading . . . .

That fluttering kicked up to a hammering against her ribcage as Ives strolled into view. How could she possibly go anywhere that would mean leaving this feeling behind her?

She found herself drifting closer to the window, her forehead pressing to the glass sooner than she realized.

She watched as he sat down in front of Cassius. Watched as Cassius closed the book and looked up at the other man. She could only imagine what they were chatting about.

Clearly, the topic was troubling, as Cassius unexpectedly slammed down his book and shot to his feet. The suddenness of his movement actually caused Violet to jump in place.

But Ives was standing just as fast. He shot out his hand, latching his fingers around Cassius' elbow to prevent him from storming away.

Their apparent arguing continued, but then there was another sudden movement and—

Violet's jaw fell and she thought her heart had stopped in her chest. They'd closed the distance between them, and now they were . . . .

Kissing?

She wanted to pretend that she was not seeing what she was seeing, even as the thought of it set off a pooling warmth low in her body. She wanted to tell herself she was misreading the action, that they were only talking *very* close together, and she was seeing them from an angle that made the interaction easy to misinterpret.

But she knew that wasn't so . . . .

Stranger still, the image sent a dozen fuzzy recollections—already a little clearer than before —through her head.

She'd seen them kiss before, in one of those sordid dreams she tried to deny having. It had been far too simple for her to take refuge in the vague dimness of what she recalled that she'd convinced herself she must be misremembering whatever images and sensations she *did* recall.

∞∞∞

She awoke sitting up. Ives stood before her, holding her hand. Before she could even ask, he was gently tugging her to her feet.

Stepping behind her as he placed his hands over her hips, he guided her to stand in front her mirror. He caught her gaze over her shoulder in the reflection. How was it possible he was even more striking in the moonlight and shadows cast through the window than he was in daylight?

"I apologize if this makes you shy," he said, brushing back her hair to move his lips along the side of her throat as he spoke, "and may sound far too-bold of me, but I quite fancy the idea of watching us this way."

Violet couldn't bring herself to answer. She was both entranced by their reflection and enjoying too much the sweep of his hands over her as he brought one up to cup her breast, and trailed the other beneath her nightdress. She knew she should feel shy, or ashamed, but she simply did not.

Not even as she felt his fingers dip between her thighs. Nor as he pushed his hips forward against hers, causing her to rock against his stroking hand.

Not even as she noticed, in the reflection . . . . Cassius sat on the edge of the bed, lazily reclined on an elbow as he watched them.

He uttered a hungry sound as his gaze traveled over the pair before the mirror. "Not even certain I should help."

Ives chuckled, as though that were a response. The girl shivered as he dragged his teeth along the pulse in her throat and he tightened his arms around her, pressing her closer to him, still.

"There is something to be said for voyeurism, after all, I suppose," the man on the bed said with a grin.

Ives did speak this time, chuckling again as his fingers teased and toyed. "I do so enjoy the little noises that she makes, don't you?"

Biting into his bottom lip, Cassius nodded. "Music to my ears, in fact."

She jumped then, even as the hand between her thighs stroked faster, edging her toward the sweet bliss of release. There'd been that pinch at her throat that she dimly recalled happening before.

Yet . . . somehow the sensation of Ives' mouth working her skin, of the tip of his tongue swirling over her pulse, added to the sweet, tingling ache he was causing with his fingertips.

She was tensing against him and he helped her, holding her up on her toes to force her muscles to go taut all the quicker.

Violet found she couldn't help herself, her gaze locked on the reflection of the other man as the orgasm tore through her.

"Bloody hell," he said, his head shaking. He seemed to be laughing at himself as he stood from the bed and crossed to them.

Cassius held her dreamy gaze for a moment. But then Ives lifted his head. In the reflection . . . there appeared a splash of crimson on his lips in the darkness. Cassius lapped at Ives' lips, licking them clean before covering the other man's mouth with his own.

The rumbling sounds of satisfaction they each

made were right there in her ear while she watched them, still, in the mirror.

As the sweet warmth spiraling through her began to ebb, her body relaxing in response, Ives started rocking her against his hand, once more.

He broke the kiss and tipped his head away, allowing for Cassius to press his lips to Violet's throat.

The last thing she recalled before drifting off was the press of Cassius' body in front of her, pushing her more tightly against Ives. He lapped and suckled gently at her skin, much as Ives had moments earlier.

∞∞∞

Violet snapped back to the moment. Surely, only the space of a few heartbeats had ticked by, but . . . .

There they were, down in the garden, kissing. She *had* seen it before, but that was not possible!

Her fingers scrambled at the side of her throat, looking for some sign of what that pinching sensation had been. Some scrape or cut to explain the splash of crimson she'd dreamed on Ives' lips.

There was nothing . . . .

Of course there was nothing, she thought, prepared to reprimand herself. The gloominess of the house, the seclusion, they'd combined in her head to make her imagine wild notions about the men who lived here, as though they were creatures out of some dark fairy story! Some chemistry she must've witnessed between them had clearly triggered her to imagine them kissing *before* the intimate moment she was spying just now.

Yes, she thought. Violet nodded to herself even as she backpedaled from the window on trembling footsteps.

She was imagining things. Seclusion, gloominess, separation from her family . . . her feelings toward her employers. . . . All these things were combining to give her fits of hysteria.

It was an uncomfortable notion, but again she nodded. Uncomfortable, but *sensible*. She would simply make an appointment with the closest doctor straight away so she could have the matter *seen to*.

As though she could not help herself, she leaned toward the window, again, sneaking one last glance at them. They were just breaking away from that kiss, their breathing heavy as they stood —their foreheads pressed together, Ives' hand curved around the back of Cassius' neck in a gentle hold.

Yes, an appointment with a doctor, she thought, again. Because if she could not collect herself, there was no way she could continue on here, what with them doing such things and having private chats about how they were each falling in love with her.

∞∞∞

"Did she see?"

Cassius flicked his gaze up toward the window. From his vantage point, he had a clear view of her staring out into the gardens, but knew she would not be able to determine the direction in which he was looking. Inhaling deep through his nostrils, he watched as she turned away from the window.

"Yes. She's gone, now."

Lifting his head, Ives nodded. "Good, because I'm not quite finished with you, yet."

Cassius followed along, a smile on his lips, as Ives dragged him by his wrist into the depths of the garden.

Chapter Nine

Questions and Contentment

I ves' pen stilled against the document on his desk. Arching a brow, he lifted his attention to Violet. She stood in the open doorway of his study, her gaze on the hem of her skirts as she twisted her fingers in front of her.

After what she'd witnessed from that window in the old wing yesterday afternoon, he'd expected she might ask many things. A request to see a doctor, herself, was nowhere among them.

Setting aside his work, he watched her for a moment. She didn't look feverish or pale, nor did her respiration seem labored. Nevertheless, the abruptness of her request worried him.

"Are you not feeling well, Violet?"

The concern in his voice startled her, and she couldn't help but lift her gaze to meet his. As always, his handsome features were a sweet torment to her sensibilities that stole her breath for a moment. Dear Lord . . . she'd been here for a month, already, and saw the man literally every bloody day. *When* would she grow accustomed to him?

"Oh, I'm feeling fine, I just . . . ." God, how could she tell him what was wrong with her?

His brow furrowing, he pushed away from his desk and stood. "You can tell me. You know that, don't you?"

The young woman swallowed hard as she nodded. "I suppose, but it's not really—"

"Don't think of me as your employer right now, not if it's preventing you from being wholly truthful with me." Rounding the desk, he crossed the floor to stand before her. "Think of me as your friend."

Again she nodded. Though, it turned out to be a struggle to get the words to form, the syllables feeling quite stuck in her throat, just now. "I, um . . . I think perhaps I am not adjusting to the country air as well as one would think. Those strange dreams I mentioned to you before have returned, and well . . . ."

Ives' broad shoulders drooped as he looked down at her. In what he knew she'd consider a bold move, he gathered both of her hands into his own, his grip firm but gentle.

"Well?" he echoed, frowning thoughtfully.

His fingers were so warm, wrapped around hers like this. She knew she should not tell him what had been happening in her head, because no matter how he put it, he *was* her employer. But she wanted to tell him, at least something of it, anyway.

Dear Lord. If Fletcher or Grace knew she was falling in love with her employers—*plural*, as she had the regrettable misfortune of having become besotted with both of them—and had not resigned her post, they'd have her in a sanitarium for such an un-Violet-like decision faster than she could blink!

"I feel like I've been imagining things that simply cannot be, mad things, unspeakable things. Things that *never* would have occurred to me merely a month ago. And, so ... the only reason I can think that I might be experiencing such imaginings is that, well ... I believe I'm having hysterics." She felt her cheeks flame as the last word left her lips in a rushed, airy whisper.

She'd not meant to blurt all that out so candidly.

Ives' eyebrows shot up. "Oh?" He chuckled and shook his head. "I doubt that to be so. You are very level-headed and logical and do not at all seem prone to—"

"Ives? Please." Running the tip of her tongue

along her suddenly parched lips in a nervous gesture, she gave a head shake of her own. She would ignore the strange notion in the back of her mind that he was charmed by her flustered state. "I'm imagining things that are . . . unhealthy of a *proper young lady*."

Somehow, his brows managed to climb higher, still. "I see."

"So, yes. I . . . require an appointment with the nearest local doctor, soon as one can be arranged, thank you."

"No, you don't."

Her eyes shot wide at the quickness and fluidity of his dismissal. "What?"

He tightened his hands around hers, a quiet sigh escaping him. "I'll not bore you with my reasons now, but I will say it is *my* opinion that a young woman is entitled to imagine a great many things for which society dictates she should be ashamed, or that she's gone mad. However, if my honest thought on the matter is not enough to assure you, I would like to remind you I *do* have medical training, and am perfectly aware of the treatment for hysteria."

She felt warmth flood her cheeks all over again as she stared up at him in silence.

"If you like, Violet," he said, his tone as gentle as his hands around hers, "I could administer it and save on your need to visit some stranger. However . . . ." He let his voice trail off as he pursed his lips, rather suddenly appearing deep in thought.

Yes, that *was* what she'd believed he was suggesting. She could scarcely think around the idea of Ives handling such a delicate and *intimate* problem. Forcing a gulp down her throat, the question tumbled breathless from her lips, "However?"

A troubled expression flickered across his features as he held her gaze. "I am fully aware that when a doctor delivers such treatment, he is expected to maintain a level of clinical detachment from his patient."

She knew what she was seeing—she recognized the heat in his blue eyes as he stared down at her. Yet she told herself that, too, was the work of her imagination. The ruse was deliberate; necessary for her to keep her composure.

Was her mind actually playing tricks on her now, or had their bodies drifted closer together as they talked?

"I'm afraid," he said, pausing to swallow, "were you to allow me to do this for you, there is a chance I might not be able to remain clinical or detached."

There was no denying to herself, then, the way her pulse quickened and her body flushed as she thought about Ives reacting to such a thing. Yet, she was uncertain whether she was frightened by such a prospect or intrigued.

Most likely, a bit of both.

Forcing a gulp down her throat, she managed to get her bearings, somehow. Backpedaling a step, she took a deep breath. "I . . . I need time to think about which option would be preferable, if that's all right?" She didn't mean preferable, of course—she meant *wise*, she meant *safe*, neither of which did she consider letting Lord Ives Hayward, II slip his hand between her thighs, proper procedure, or not—and she *knew* he was cognizant of her true meaning.

To his credit, he did not look regretful or angry with her for her caution. On the contrary, the small, gentle smile that curved his mouth appeared an expression of understanding.

Nodding, he gave her hands another gentle squeeze before letting her fingers slips from his as he said, "Of course. I would not wish to do anything that makes you uncomfortable, Violet."

With an unsteady smile, she nodded back.

She had another day to herself as Cassius was being moody, again, and she should really find . . . anywhere else to be right now. Though, some spontaneous fancy took hold of her senses, and she shot forward, brushing her lips against Ives' cheek in a quick, feathery touch.

The action had *nothing* to do with the sudden rush of tingly warmth through her as she remembered witnessing Cassius and Ives kissing, she insisted to herself.

Just as fast, she pulled back and turned on her heel. She was already striding down the corridor by the time her senses caught up with her and the responding heat filled her face for the third time in what could not have been more than five minutes passing.

She didn't notice the way Ives ducked his head through the open doorway to watch her go. Didn't see the somewhat wicked half-grin that curved his lips, nor the captivated gleam in his eyes as his gaze trailed her movements, watching her until she disappeared beyond the curve of the staircase landing.

∞∞∞

The gardens of Winterbury Hall were gorgeous, but they were also expansive. Violet thought it was just her luck that she'd gotten herself lost. Sighing, she turned her head and looked about her lush surroundings. It really did serve her right, didn't it? With another day to do as she pleased, perhaps she should've gone back to work in the old wing, yet . . . .

Her shoulders drooped. This had been a poor decision. After what she'd seen through the window yesterday, perhaps she shouldn't be out here. What if the gardens were some special place for the two of them?

Swallowing hard, she shook her head at herself and started off in a random direction—each time she set off in what she thought was the correct one, she ended up more turned around than before, so random seemed safer. She still wasn't certain how she felt about that private moment she had spied, about what it must mean.

Well . . . that wasn't wholly true. She knew how it made her feel *physically*, but emotionally? She was at a loss. A confused, jumbled loss. She'd overheard Ives and Cassius' conversation yesterday morning. She knew what they felt for her . . . .

She was aware of the meaning behind the intensity in Cassius' look when their gazes met lately, despite how often she insisted to herself she was mistaken. She knew what fueled the tone of Ives' voice as he'd spoken to her in his study doorway; she knew what caused that possessive grip of his hands around hers and the flickering warmth in his eyes, even as she refused to believe it possible.

But if the men *were* a couple, what did that mean for what they felt toward her? Violet chewed at her lower lip as she walked. This was more confusing than the plot of one of those frivolous, absurdly romantic novels with which Grace was so taken. If they'd not been so open as to discuss their feelings for her with one another, if they'd kept things to themselves and she'd found out some other way, she'd understand. But they knew and they carried on, still?

Her footfalls drew to a halt and she pulled in a deep breath. What if that was what they were arguing about yesterday? They'd gotten into that heated discussion before they'd kissed . . . .

Could it have been about her?

Shaking her head, she let that breath out in an exasperated huff. "Oh, listen to yourself! That could've been about anything—they've had near their entire lives together before *you* came along, Violet Ramsey! Probably a matter of coincidental timing that had *nothing* to do with you, at all."

The sentiment was bracing, a bit disheartening, yet probably the reality of it all. And try as she might, she could not bring herself to believe a word of it.

Gathering her skirts in her hands, she picked up her pace. At this rate, she'd be wandering about out here until after dark. Oh, yes, the rattled emotions that would result from giving Ives and Cassius a fright when she turned up missing for dinner was certainly not going to improve her situation, or clear any confusion.

Much to her surprise, however, the next turn in the path beneath her feet brought the estate house into view. With a sigh, she nodded as she continued along. She should really have someone take her on a proper tour of the garden grounds in the near future—something that possibly should've happened sooner, but had simply been glossed over, somehow.

As she got close to the house, she noticed something so sweetly innocent, she could not help an airy and surprised giggle.

A smile playing on her lips, she approached the white-seated tree swing. She reached out tentatively, pulling on the ropes. They were sturdy, which seemed promising, given their weathered condition, making it even more unexpected that the white lacquer on the wood hadn't peeled away. It didn't show more age than some minor bubbling. Perhaps it had been replaced, but the ropes left as they were due to how hearty they turned out?

Oh, good Lord! Why must you examine absolutely *everything?* Her inner voice scolded her while she rounded the swing and seated herself carefully.

With a mildly self-deprecating snicker, she shook her head at her thoughts. As she started swinging, keeping the motions small and gentle, she considered that her life was in a very odd place right now. She'd never had a position in which she was so genuinely unsure of what the day ahead would be like when she awoke each morning.

She couldn't even say if that was a bad thing or a good one, however. Yes, she spent equal amounts of time teaching as she was hired to as she did *not*. Yes, she was slowly but surely falling in love with both her employer and her student. Yes, she had fleeting and hazy memories of steamy, *highly* inappropriate dreams about both of them—memories that had honestly made her wonder if dark creatures of myth could be real for a ridiculous moment. Yes, that she was not more concerned about either of those things had her worrying for her mental state. Yes, there might even be a ghost lurking somewhere in that house, and she barely believed in ghosts.

A wistful sigh escaping her lips, she fixed her gaze on the house. So many things that should've made her leave this place, and yet . . . she was strangely content here.

"I see you found my hiding spot."

Violet's heart skipped a beat at the sound of Cassius' voice behind her. He wrapped his hands around the ropes just over hers, slowing her momentum.

She didn't look back at him as she spoke. "You sound like you're feeling better."

He hummed a quick, thoughtful sound as he started swinging her gently. "I suppose I am."

"Well, then, it is still early in the afternoon." Despite her willingness to make the suggestion, she was rather certain she already knew what the young man's answer would be. "We could get back to some of your lessons. I'm afraid I'm woefully neglecting your education as of late."

"Oh, I don't know that I'm feeling *that* much better."

She shook her head, laughing. "Somehow I knew you'd say that."

He caught and held her, stopping the swinging rather abruptly. When she tipped back her head to meet his gaze, he answered with a small, suspicious grin on his lips. "Then why bother with the offer?"

Violet shrugged, marveling at how hard it

was to stay angry with him. She should be furious he was so flippant about this opportunity to gain a proper education, but instead, she found herself sympathizing. She couldn't know what this transition was like for him, but she could imagine that adjusting to formal lessons was not as simple as it seemed from the perspective of one who already possessed said education.

"Perhaps I was hoping you would surprise me."

Snickering, he shook his head at her. He didn't respond, only starting to push the swing, once more.

With a slip of a grin, she returned her gaze to the building before them. She immediately gasped, giving a little start.

Again, he stopped her motions. "What is it?"

The young woman sighed, pressing her palm over her heart as she willed her jumping pulse to steady. "I . . . saw someone in the window and it frightened me, is all. But I suppose it must've been Ives."

"Oh, so you find him scary, do you? I suppose that makes two of us."

Laughing in spite of herself, Violet gave his fingers around the rope a delicate, playful swat. "That's not what I meant. I didn't expect to see him in the old wing. He gave me the impression he doesn't go in there at all if he can help it."

A troubled frown marring his features, Cassius stepped around the swing to stand before her.

"He *doesn't*."

"Oh?" Her mahogany eyes wide, she looked from him to the window in question, and back. "Then Gilbert, perhaps? Though I could swear the person was dark-haired."

His brows pinched together. "Gilbert doesn't go in there, either. He only stays in the portions of the house where Ives might have need of him."

Swallowing hard, she shook her head as she held his gaze. "Then whom did I just see?"

Cassius squared his shoulders as he held out his hand to her. "Let's go find out, shall we?"

Chapter Ten

The Witch's Ghost

She wanted to think the house felt different as she walked up the stairs toward the third-floor, Cassius' hand secure around hers. That it felt larger and darker and colder, but she knew better. That was her imagination trying to run away with her, and hadn't she already appeared foolish in front of Ives with that nonsense over the physician's skeleton in the old doctor's office? The last thing she needed was to overreact in front of Cassius, too. Whatever feelings might be developing between them, she was still his instructor, and could certainly do without anything that might undermine that dynamic.

She was ignoring wholly that said dynamic was already assailed by myriad inappropriate circumstances, but one flutter of the heart at a time.

As they reached the third-floor landing, he turned her in the direction of the old wing. She tried not to put too much consideration into the way he walked half a step behind her. It was surely only her imagination, again, that he seemed to want to place his free hand on her waist as he guided her along. Only her imagination that he might want to stop her and pull her back against him.

Oh, dear God, *Violet! There you go again.* She halted mid-step, forcing a breath. The very idea of being that close to him set off a flood of warmth in her cheeks.

"Are you all right?" he asked, those usually playful blue eyes of his showing concern. "You look a bit flushed."

Holding his gaze a moment, she nodded. "Yes, I'm sorry. Let's keep moving."

With a nod of his own in return, Cassius started them moving through the old wing, once more. "Now, which room do you think you saw the person?"

"Further along." She jutted her chin toward the very last door before the bend in the corridor. "That one, I think."

"I understand you had an adventure in the doctor's office shortly after you first arrived here."

Violet glanced at his face, her shoulders drooping. "I was hoping Ives had kept that to himself."

"Well," Cassius began, arching a brow as he shrugged, "I think he could hardly help it. Seemed to find the incident endearing."

All right, Ives *had* slipped and called her *darling* after that, so she'd imagine that yes, he had found it endearing. Even so . . . . "As I said, I had *hoped* he'd not passed that along. Regardless, it was not just after I arrived. It was that evening when you and I returned from the museum."

Cassius nodded, frowning pensively while they walked. She thought perhaps it was her increasingly detrimental imagination that his expression was one of dawning realization. As though her clarification caused something to suddenly make sense for him.

Yet, that in itself didn't make sense to her, so she pushed it aside.

When they reached the door, he pulled her to a halt. Sidestepping to stand before her, he deliberately captured her gaze with his own. "I see. So, it's fine for him to witness you having a vulnerable, completely human moment, but not for *me*?"

"Well, yes."

His brows shot up.

Shaking her head, she frowned. "I mean, no. That's not what I meant. I am your teacher, Cassius. It matters how you see me, how you think of me." Oh, damn, but that wasn't really what she wanted to say, either.

Sooner than she could attempt to correct herself, Cassius spoke, offering a quizzical half-smile. "So how he sees you doesn't matter?"

Her brown eyes widening as she held his gaze, she seemed to fold in on herself a bit. "You're confusing me on purpose, which I don't very much appreciate, and I'd really like not to discuss this any further, thank you!"

Again with that infuriatingly easy shrug of his, he nodded. "As you wish." Turning back toward the door, he tried the knob and pushed it open.

Violet felt uneasy the instant the hinges let out their first whining creak. She'd not been in this room, yet, so she had no idea what awaited them.

Stepping inside, she looked about the dusty old suite. Possibly a guest room? But then her gaze fell upon the portrait gracing the far wall. An elegant woman with olive features and a mass of ebony hair stared back at her. Her equally dark eyes were enormous and somehow unnerving.

"Who's that?"

This time, Cassius did step up directly behind Violet. She could feel the weight of his hands resting on her waist and the tickle of his breath against her skin as he breathed.

"I'm not terribly familiar with this portrait, exactly, but I've heard about that woman. Isabeau Mercier."

Violet felt frozen in place, her gaze oddly

stuck on that of the women in the painting. "Isabeau Mercier?" she repeated in a whisper. What a beautiful name.

"I'm actually surprised there's a likeness of her anywhere in Winterbury Hall."

"Why is that?" Violet wanted to turn her head and look at him, but she was a bit afraid to with how close his face was to hers.

"Well, for one thing, she's not really called by her name. Instead, the poor dear managed to earn the title of 'The Mad Witch.'"

In that moment, Violet wasn't certain what had her pulse quickening more. There was the ominous tone in which he'd spoken . . . and then there was the feeling of his breath against her neck, of his lips brushing her skin. As though he'd lowered his mouth to the side of her throat, pausing mid-kiss, just long enough to answer.

Her eyes drifted closed and she found herself leaning back against him. The movement felt strangely natural, entirely involuntary. "What did she do to earn such a title?" Somehow, she knew, the discussion was part of whatever play was going on here between them. She wanted to pull away, wanted to leave the room, wanted to reprimand Cassius for being so very familiar with her . . . . And yet, at the same time, wanted to do *none* of those things, at all. Wanted only to stand here like this in his embrace, feeling the warm press of his lips below her ear.

He made a deep, rumbling sound in the back

of his throat as he sighed, grinning when his breath against her skin made her shiver in his arms. "Well, aside from—as the story goes—actually *being* a witch?"

She swallowed hard, tipping back her head to rest against his shoulder. "I mean . . . what did she actually do? What is her story?" This was all so dreadfully inappropriate, she should really stop him . . . .

Cassius grazed her earlobe ever so lightly with his teeth, uttering a wicked little laugh at the sigh that escaped her. "Well, it's said that she came to Winterbury Hall at the behest of Ives' mother, the Lady Beryl Hayward. Beryl was apparently fascinated with spirits and the otherworldly—in a way that probably would've seen her hanged or burned at the stake two centuries ago. This was, of course, all before Ives was born."

Violet found herself curling backward to lean tighter against him. She rested her arms over his as he slid his hands around her waist to hold her there. "So Beryl knew Isabeau was a witch already?"

Chuckling, he shrugged, dropping another kiss to her throat. "Well, I'm certain it probably wasn't all that openly advertised, but yes. She summoned Isabeau to perform a séance. Wanted to speak to her . . . mother, I think? Of course, I'm certain the *who* is not really important. It's said that Beryl became enamored of Isabeau and invited her here frequently. For longer and longer stays each time."

Violet's brows shot up. "Oh? Were they ... ?"

"Lovers?" Again, he shrugged. "That is the rumor, though it was never confirmed. Does the thought of such a thing—someone taking a lover of the same gender—make you uncomfortable?"

She seemed painfully aware of the rise and fall of his chest against her back as he breathed. Of the warmth of him—unusual, given how chilled he typically felt—wrapped around her. The question prompted her to remember the kiss she'd witnessed between him and Ives in the garden.

And the kiss she'd dreamed seeing them share just before he'd pressed his lips to her throat and—

"No," she said, continuing the conversation in a deliberate bid to distract herself from the impossible thing that same dream had shown her. Sharp teeth and blood, yet her own unmarked flesh told her that was the work of her imagination, alone, even if that kiss *had* been proven to have a basis in reality. "Should it?"

"I would think opinions on whether or not it should vary based on the person to whom you're speaking, but *I* find it refreshing, actually." Again, he caught her earlobe in a delicate bite before going on. "Shall I continue?"

She wasn't certain as to what he was referring. "You ... you mean with the story?"

His arms tightened around her as he laughed. "Yes. I'll pretend I don't know what else you *think* I could mean."

Violet was painfully aware of the blush in her cheeks as she realized he'd caught her imagining where this moment between them might lead if it went further than embraces and lips against *appropriately* bared skin. Yet, she couldn't help herself. She didn't know what had gotten hold of her senses, but as much as she knew this was woefully *in*appropriate, she also had to battle a troubling impression that this moment would be 'complete', were Ives present.

Damnable dreams of hers!

"As—as you were saying?" she said, forcing out the words.

He smirked, nodding. "Yes. As I was saying . . . . If they *were* lovers, Isabeau had a funny way of showing it, as not far after she was visiting with Beryl so long the servants whispered the witch had moved in, Beryl took ill. This portrait's commissioning, I'd imagine, only served to validate such rumors about their relationship. But, as I said, Beryl took ill. And it seemed no matter what the estate's doctor did, she would not get better, nor could he understand what ailed her enough to even make a proper diagnosis."

Violet forgot her own refusal to turn her face to his earlier and immediately found his mouth before hers. He traced her lips with the tip of his tongue. Pulling away just enough to meet her gaze, he exhaled sharply, his breath making the soft, damp skin tingle.

"Go on," she prompted in an airy whisper.

His eyes searched her face as he asked, "With the story?"

Swallowing hard, she reminded herself to breathe. "I'll pretend I don't know what else you think I could mean."

A lopsided grin curved his mouth. "You do catch on quick. All right. The only time Beryl's health seemed to improve was when Isabeau was here. Sure enough, every time Isabeau returned to the city, Beryl's health declined. And, given there was still no illness the doctor could find . . . ."

"They called it witchcraft."

"They called it witchcraft," he echoed, his tone thoughtful. "They believed Isabeau had cursed her, trying to make Beryl dependent on her constant companionship. And so, the next time Isabeau visited . . . well, we actually have no idea what happened to her. She was never seen again. Beryl got healthier, but never *truly* recovered—either from the heartbreak or the illness is anyone's guess. Only a year or so after Ives was born, her body just . . . gave out. So 'witch' because, well, she was one, and 'mad' because to inflict that sort of torment on the one you love simply to keep yourself useful is hardly sane, now is it?"

"Clearly not. So . . . did Ives' father kill Isabeau?"

"No one was ever able to prove anything, but one would assume so."

"I remember Ives telling me," she said, aware

how strange it should seem to her that they were having this conversation with their faces so close together, their lips brushed with every word spoken, "that it was after his mother died his father refused to let anyone use this wing. This must've been ... must've been where Isabeau stayed."

"I think you might be right. I ask again, are you certain this is the room where you saw the person at the window?"

She nodded.

He nipped at her bottom lip. "Could it be that you glimpsed the portrait?"

Violet forced her head to turn, looking from the window to the framed likeness of Isabeau, before returning her attention to Cassius. "Not possible. The angle is all wrong. No ...." She tried to imagine she didn't feel a sudden chill up her spine as a corner of her mind wandered.

"No?"

"This is going to sound *completely* mad, but the night I found my way into the old doctor's office, I had seen something. Like the shape of a person, yet not. That was what led me there. I hadn't told Ives, but I had witnessed a similar ... apparition, I suppose, just earlier that morning in the corridor outside this room. Nearly in the same place. Now *this?* With Ives and Gilbert never coming in here, and you and I being the only other two people in the estate besides them ... ?"

"Are you suggesting you think you've seen

Isabeau's *ghost*?"

Her shoulders drooped as she finally pulled out of his embrace to turn and face him. The moment of near-sinful warmth between them had evaporated in the wake of her confession. But he only stared back at her, his blue eyes narrowed and calculating as he waited for her to answer. "As I said, it sounds *completely* mad, I know, but—"

"But they never *did* find her body," Cassius finished for her in a hushed voice, tearing his gaze from hers to dart about the floor as he thought. "It ... it does sound completely mad, yes. But what if it is true?"

"I ... I'm not sure what to think, Cassius."

"Maybe we had best to keep this to ourselves, for now. Ives doesn't like discussing Isabeau Mercier. He blames her for his mother's death, after all." He frowned, shaking his head. That playful, too-familiar side of him was all but gone now, even as he caught her hand in his. "Perhaps we should discuss this somewhere a bit *less* sad and dusty, hmm?"

Nodding, she let him lead her from the depressing guest suite. Out in the corridor with the door to the witch's room closed behind them, she already felt bit better.

Yet, her heart leapt into her throat when they neared the landing, coming face-to-face with Ives as he climbed the stairs.

Violet and Cassius both halted. They watched as Ives' gaze took in each of them and then their joined hands, in turn, before looking to both of them, again.

She wasn't entirely certain how to feel at the sudden, sharp coolness in Ives' typically warm gaze. It was likely only her imagination, but she would have sworn the temperature of the very air around them had dropped as they stood there waiting for him to speak.

Finally, squaring his shoulders and offering a mirthless grin, Ives asked, "Shall I even dare to wonder what you two have been up to?"

Chapter Eleven

A Fine Day for Hysterics

Violet winced, standing just before the third-floor landing beside Cassius. He had yet to relinquish his hold on her hand, his fingers tangled with hers throughout a reluctant explanation to Ives. She had been at a loss for precisely what to say as she'd stared back at the master of the house, given Cassius' advisement of not mentioning anything about Isabeau to Ives. Cassius, on the other hand, seemed to take her sudden panic into account, his tone almost dismissive of Ives' anger as he relayed someone seeing the figure of a dark-haired person through the window.

Only . . . he claimed *he* was the one to have glimpsed the specter.

Ives only seemed more aggravated, not less, by Cassius' reasoning. His shoulders sloping downward, he'd stepped past them and stalked down the corridor of the old wing. Violet exchanged a quick glance with the younger man, though she could not quite make sense of the look in his eyes, whilst they hurried after him.

As she observed Ives crossing the floor, his gaze roving over the painting as an expression of disgust twisted his beautiful face, she couldn't help but remember being so very close with Cassius only moments earlier not at all far from where they stood, now. Watching Ives turn to pace to the window where Cassius had claimed to have seen the figure standing, the remembered sensation of Cassius' body against hers and his lips brushing her throat stole her breath.

Worse, she could feel Cassius' attention on her from the corner of his eye. Though she wouldn't turn her head to look at him just now, she felt sure there was the tiniest half-grin tugging at his mouth.

When Ives spun back to face them, Violet jumped a little at the abruptness of the movement. Only then did she realize the other man's fingers were still locked with hers. And, from the brief downward flicker of Ives' gaze, she knew he'd registered that continued hold, as well.

Swallowing hard, the lord dropped his eyes from the pair. He shook his head, appearing to collect himself before speaking. "I recall when we were younger, Cassius. When you weren't having an episode, you were quite the merry prankster." His features pinched in exasperation. "I had hoped you'd outgrown that rather immature trait. Regardless, I never thought you would try such a thing on Violet."

Cassius' eyes shot wide at the accusation. "What? Ives, no! I didn't—"

"Of all the things you could do," Ives went on through clenched teeth, fussing to straighten his collar and the cuffs of his jacket—minutia to focus on as he gathered his temper—as though Cassius hadn't said a word, "I *never* imagined you would—"

"It wasn't Cassius who saw it," Violet blurted out, as much to calm Ives' anger as to spare Cassius being blamed for something that wasn't true. "It was me."

The shift in Ives' demeanor was instant. The tense set of his shoulders eased and his fussing fingertips stilled. Those piercing blue eyes of his locked on her face as he let his arms drop to his sides. She could swear the flicker through them then was of one feeling wounded.

The idea that the unwilling deception had hurt him tugged painfully at her heart.

Shrugging, she elaborated before he could ask why she'd allowed Cassius to lie for her. "He was only trying to keep me from appearing foolish in front of you. I hadn't . . . hadn't known what to say, because he told me how much you dislike discussing anything about, well, *her*."

"And you thought I would not believe you?"

Forcing a gulp down her throat, she dropped her gaze from his. "Given our conversation in your study earlier, I should think it evident that I'm not sure I believe myself. But I did think I saw someone up here, I *truly* did."

When silence rang through the room, she forced herself to return her attention to his face. He appeared deep in thought over something. After another moment of silence as they stared at one another, he nodded, his expression grave.

"Time to help you sort what's real and what is your imagination, I should think."

Crossing the room, he reached out, his fingers closing on the wrist of Violet's free hand. He stepped around Cassius and started tugging her along behind him as he made his way back down the corridor.

At the sensation of his fingers disentangling from hers, she looked back at him over her shoulder. Strangely, she felt more aware of Cassius' hand on hers in its absence. He offered her an apologetic look, staying right where she'd left him. Whatever Ives had in mind just now, she knew the other man was quite aware it did not involve him.

Swallowing hard, she turned her attention forward. Ives continued guiding her along the corridor, out of the old wing entirely, past the mouth of the staircase. Without so much as a word or a backward glance at her, he opened the door to his study and ushered her inside.

She was distinctly cognizant of him releasing his hold on her wrist. Distinctly cognizant of the sound of the door closing behind them.

Feeling silently prompted, she stepped further into the room. Once she stood at the center, she halted and turned to face him. Somehow, seeing that he'd removed his jacket and was placing it gently aside on his desk caused her breath to catch in her throat.

He performed a preliminary exam. The process was typical, familiar, and completed quickly, passing for Violet in something of a blur. She was aware of Ives' fingertips, gentle on her throat to check her pulse, of his ear far too close to her breast to listen to her breathing. Of his palms cupping her jaw to tip back her head, peering into her eyes.

"Breathing and heart rate normal," he murmured, seemingly to himself. "Eyes clear, skin temperate to the touch."

But then he let go and backpedaled, and she felt strangely off-kilter standing on her own two feet. It seemed only by the barest good fortune that she maintained her balance with minimal effort.

"Find someplace comfortable, please." He wasn't looking at her as he unclasped his cuff links and set them aside, as well. His expression was entirely blank, nearly cold as he started rolling his sleeves up to his elbows.

Her eyes shot wide as she realized he *truly* meant to do this. Even as she moved to follow his command, looking about the room to find a suitable spot before going to the chaise lounge against the far wall, she said, "Just earlier you told me you'd let me think about this."

"Yes, well, that was before what you *thought* you saw in that room."

She swallowed hard once more, trying to get her breathing under control as she seated herself and turned to lay back. Blinking rapidly, she stared up at the ceiling, trying not to think on the idea of his hand slipping under her skirts, or what it was going to feel like to have his fingers stroking against her. Honestly, she only tried to think how fortuitous it was that she wasn't wearing a crinoline dress, or this matter would be a touch more complicated than simply laying back.

"Are you comfortable?" he asked, his voice sounding both unflustered and strained at all once —as though he was trying for that clinical detachment he'd mentioned earlier and struggling to maintain it.

Closing her eyes, she nodded. "I again mention that you said you'd leave this to be *my* choice."

"I had every intention of doing so," he said as he pulled a chair over and sat beside the chaise.

"But this . . . sighting of yours troubles me."

"So you *do* think my imagination has been running away with me?" She tried for a neutral tone, but still she could hear the hurt in her own words.

He arched a brow, his gaze snapping up to lock on her face. "I did not say that. But, as I *did* say, this sighting troubles me."

She sank her teeth into her lower lip as she tried to focus her attention on the ceiling above her. Tried and failed, her eyes dropping to meet his while he carefully pushed her skirts out of his way.

Oh, this was nerve wracking!

"I'm troubled, because I was raised to respect superstition. I know that probably seems out of character with how you've come to think of me." The whisper of fabric was audible as he parted her legs, the opening in her undergarment falling wider with the movement. "I have never experienced a sighting, myself, but I will not be wholly dismissive of the possibility, either."

She jumped a little at the first brush of his hand between her thighs. Already she could feel her face flushing, the skin of her cheeks tingling with warmth as his fingertips slid against her.

He went on, that almost-detachment in his voice while he stroked her gently. "As such, we must do this so that your head is clear. But I want you to be alert at all times after this. If you have another sighting, or cannot dismiss the one you just had, we will know it's not something easily pushed aside as some manifestation of hysterics."

Violet could tell he was working her up slowly. She didn't know if she was grateful that he was not simply hurrying through the treatment, or horrified that he was *not* being cold and clinical and simply rushing her to climax.

She pressed her lips into a line as she nodded, trembling as he quickened his pace just a bit.

"Tell me, then" he said, as though they were carrying on a conversation over tea. "This was not the first time you experienced something here."

The young woman shook her head. She found herself fighting not to move against his fingertips. He was trying to remain detached, she should do him the courtesy of not responding to his treatment wantonly.

"Tell me about what you've seen?" His fingers pressed a bit harder.

Her breath caught in her throat and she lost the battle with herself. Her head fell back a little as she shivered, her hips rocking of their own volition. "The night . . . . The night I stumbled upon the doctor's office, I believe I was lured there, somehow."

"Oh?" Again, he quickened his pace a hint, his fingertips pressing more firmly as they rubbed over the slick skin. "I remember you telling me you believed you had seen something. Describe what happened."

"I was . . . ." Her voice trailed off and she

struggled a moment to focus on her breathing. "I was walking up the stairs after having returned home from the museum with Cassius. And when I . . . when I looked up, there appeared a figure. It was staring down at me from beyond the railing, but it was all in shadow. The way it leaned down, I should've been able to see who it was clearly, but it was all black."

"Were you not terrified?"

There was another sound of rustling fabric and she looked down. Ives had placed the arm of his free hand out before her, his palm braced against the cushion. She couldn't seem to care anymore if he thought poorly of her or admonished her later for her movements, pushing herself more tightly against the working of his fingers as she reached out, clamping her hands around his forearm.

Dear Lord, she was so acutely aware of his gaze still on her face.

"I was, but I chose to be logical about it." She forced her mouth shut to keep in a keening moan as she felt her limbs starting to tense. Drawing in a gulp of air, she continued in a breathless whisper. "I had glimpsed it that morning, as well, but only for a moment. I followed the shadow to prove to myself that it was nothing at all. My imagination and lack of sleep; I didn't—didn't want it to be anything more."

Ives graciously held his tongue as she let out a moan that, if her expression was anything to go by, she'd uttered entirely in spite of herself. "And yet, it led you to the old wing?"

He moved faster, pressed a bit harder, still, and she gasped, her body going taut as he pushed her over the edge. Somehow, she managed a nod even as the orgasm tore through her.

She could sense his continued attention on her face. She thought she could hear some hushed, breathy groan from him as he watched her. Thought she felt the muscles in his forearm strain beneath her hands, as though he was trying to keep himself from reacting too strongly to her aroused state.

She didn't even care that such an observation might be wildly presumptuous of her.

As that sweet tension ebbed, he slowed his fingers. Timing his motions, he met the shivering jerking of her own body as blissful aftershocks of her orgasm rocked through her.

Swallowing hard, she shook her head as she realized how she'd responded to the treatment—precisely in the manner which she had *not* wanted. Violet caught her breath as her limbs drooped and her hands slipped from his arm.

After she stilled, he withdrew his fingers, his movements gentle as he closed her legs and pulled her skirts back into place over her. Lifting the hand that was not currently slick from working her, he wiped at her cheeks and forehead. Delicate, still, he pushed a wayward lock of her red-brown hair behind her ear as he waited for her to open her eyes.

When she did, she was greeted by the sight of that gentle, dazzling smile of his. Even as she caught her breath, still, even as she felt a blush flare in her cheeks, she could not seem to stop herself from smiling back at him.

"Based on what you've just told me," he said, his voice low and warm, "I don't believe your imagination is running anywhere, Violet. Whatever you saw led you to a history of this house about which you could not have had *any* idea."

"What are you saying?"

"Your head is clear?"

Swallowing, Violet darted her gaze about before nodding.

"And you're still *certain* you saw what you saw?"

She allowed herself a few seconds of honest deliberation before nodding. "Completely."

"I thought as much. Actually, I never stopped suspecting you were entirely of sound mind."

Her features tightened in a curious, faintly sour look. "You did? Then... then why on earth did you just—?"

Ives held up a placating hand. "Because it was what *you* needed. You were at odds with your own experiences. In your own words, you were uncertain whether or not to believe yourself. There was no way you were going to accept anyone else's belief until you had evidence you were not suffering hysterics. *Evidence* which you've just been provided."

Violet didn't know what to say to that. Yet . . . she understood he was correct. She would have gone on believing herself having hysterics —believing herself going slightly mad—as that seemed simpler, saner, more logical, than seeing a ghost—had he not helped her *clear her head*, as he'd stated the matter.

"That is why I'm saying I *believe* there is no way any of this could have been the work of your imagination." He shrugged, sighing. "I believe you truly glimpsed something in that evil woman's room. And I believe it would do this house, and everyone in it, a world of good to be rid of such a dark influence."

"You're going to search for the Mad Witch's grave?"

Now it was his turn to nod, his gaze holding hers. "If my father did kill her, if her body is somewhere on these grounds, I *shall* find it."

There was a sudden churning in the pit of Violet's stomach as she stared back at him. Something unnamable whispered to her that despite her own foolish past actions, nothing good could come from chasing the ghost of Isabeau Mercier.

As she stepped out of the study, pulling the door shut behind her, she smoothed a hand over her dress. And then promptly jumped to find Cassius lingering in the corridor.

Her skin flushed as she wondered how much he might've overheard.

His gaze flicked over her from head to foot before returning to her face. Breathing out a short, quiet laugh, he smirked.

"What?" she asked, her brows pinching together.

That mirhtful curl of his mouth widening a little, he shrugged. Turning on his heel, he started down the corridor. "Don't need medical training to administer that particular treatment." He glanced back at her over his shoulder. "I'd have gladly done it, if you'd only asked."

Her eyes widening, she only watched while he disappeared around a bend in the wall. Of all the things she'd expected today, Ives believing her about the sightings hadn't been one of them. Neither had Cassius making bold declarations that had her remembering glimpses from those wicked dreams that caused her body to heat and tingle all over again.

And he hadn't even touched her this time.

Chapter Twelve

Tears of the Damned

Over the days that followed, Violet, Cassius, Ives, and Gilbert scoured the grounds for any sign of what could potentially be an unmarked grave. Alternating between that and Cassius obligingly—if grousingly—returning to his studies, Violet did not have the time to focus too greatly on all that had gone on the day she'd glimpsed Isabeau Mercier's specter in the window.

Though she was certain that Cassius watched her from the corner of his eye when he thought she wouldn't notice, and Ives seemed even more gentle and doting with her than before—certainly more so than one should expect of someone in his station toward a person in his employ—she was grateful for the pretense that nothing had changed between her and each of them. She was wholly ignoring, of course, that the dreams had only gotten steamier, more vivid, harder to forget with the flood of morning light through her bedroom window. Some mornings she woke up with a heady moan dying on her lips.

Those mornings, she was sure she sat at breakfast with an uncontrollable blush flaring in her cheeks, certain she might've been overheard. Either she was quieter than she'd thought, or the men with whom she resided were gracious enough to not embarrass her further by alluding to hearing any ... sinful and inappropriate sounds issuing from her room during the night.

They fell into a pattern over this time. In the afternoons when they weren't working or searching, Cassius often prompted her to join him for walks in the gardens. She pretended she didn't realize how he was trying to tease her with the way his thumb traced over the inside of her wrist in delicate sweeping motions as he held her hand. He pretended he believed her obliviousness. The nights before retiring to bed saw to her sharing a drink with Ives on his study sofa, the two discussing everything and nothing at all as they stared into the dancing flames in the fireplace.

She kept account of her correspondence with Fletcher during these days, as well. Any delay seemed to worry him, and this ghost business was certainly could distract one from such mundane activities. It brightened her spirits to read that Uncle Hugh seemed happier each time they received word from her that she was safe and happy, herself. Of course, she did not divulge anything about this most recent turn of events in Winterbury Hall. If making foolish decisions based on feelings rather than logic would have her loved ones questioning her sanity, learning she was corpse-hunting in the hopes of banishing a ghost would *truly* convince them she was no longer of sound mind.

On occasion, Violet found herself feeling pulled toward the old wing. The sensation was troubling, as was the bizarre, creeping sense that she kept hearing . . . *something*. Almost a whisper, but not quiet. A soft, ephimeral murmur breathing through the air around her, the cadence making it sound like someone, very far away in a feathery little voice, was calling her name. She kept that to herself, as it only occurred when she ventured too near the old wing.

First glimpses of a previously unwitnessed specter, now hearing a voice? She didn't imagine that would go over well, even with the fact that Ives and Cassius believed her.

She could only think that Isabeau was becoming more insistent. Or was feeling more connected to her as the days ticked past. Maybe it was something to do with the witch's ghost finally feeling herself in the presence of one who might sympathize. Men were terrible at such things, even when facets of their own life mirrored another's situation.

Violet tried to look back on these moments with the sharper perspective that only came through hindsight. That day she'd first seen the shadowy figure in the old wing . . . . What was it that had drawn her gaze there? A sensation, yes. Prickling on the back of her neck. The hesitant brush of air against her ear . . . as though someone had been whispering very close to her. The remembered feeling was jarring in its sudden clarity.

Had Isabeau been whispering to her even then?

They were doing all they could to find what had become of the witch—Ives, fearing the ghost might seek to harm Violet the way she had his mother in life, was even using his influence to reach out to surrounding villages and towns in an attempt to locate any later records that made mention of the woman. Anything that might indicate that she'd slipped away from the estate grounds unseen, leaving the mystery of what had become of her almost entirely by accident.

Violet didn't like that incessant tug intent on drawing her back. Even less did she like that those hissing whispers had become more frequent as time drifted by, reaching her ears not only when she neared the old wing, but as soon as night fell, casting much of the grand house into shadow. She had an icy impression in the pit of her stomach that the portrait, itself, was somehow attempting to call to her. Quietly beckoning her to stand before it, once more. Each day she ignored it, for fear it was a work of her own subconscious . . . and perhaps a little for fear that she might find the terrifying apparition of the Mad Witch waiting for her.

Finally, after a near three weeks of fruitless searching, equally fruitless missives, more temper tantrums from Cassius than she felt any grown person should have a right to throw, and those damn dreams that she wondered might not be sapping her strength somehow—God help her, she even rushed to the mirror some mornings to check the places she felt those sweetly painful stings only to find unblemished skin—she decided there must be some resolve.

At least to *this*.

She didn't mention the dreams again. She was half-convinced they were Isabeau's work, trying to confuse her. To keep Violet transfixed with her employers enough that she would stay despite her own better judgment, yet make her question her trust in them . . . . Perhaps Isabeau was even using the dreams to syphon Violet's energy so that the specter could become strong enough to do more than just watch from windows and loom in corridors, whispering into the shadows.

Violet had paid enough attention during seances at Uncle's parties to retain at least *that* much information from the mediums in attendance. Ghosts were their strongest when they could drain energy from other sources—the living, for example, turned out to be ideal conductors for such things.

She'd laughed at herself for even forming that thought, as before she'd come to live at Winterbury Hall, she would never have given such fanficul and ludicrous beliefs the time of day.

Cassius and Ives were discussing something in hushed tones in his study, the door standing open when Violet found them. Hovering beyond the threshold, she peered in at them a moment. Dear Lord, they were so beautiful the sight of them in the same space actually caused an ache in her heart.

And an ache in a place much lower that sent a fresh wash of color to tint her cheeks. She was rather certain she'd not blushed as much in her life as she had during the near two months since she'd come here. Swallowing hard, she pushed away that notion, pushed away the memory of those dreamed sensations—Cassius' hands caressing between her thighs, Ives' lips brushing the side of her throat. Oh, even that pinching sting was something she was beginning to find exquisite . . . . She knew it was all a fantasy. Some dark, warped part of her own heart letting her find it so very tempting, though she understood how wrong it all was.

Some dark, warped part that found the dreamed memory of her blood on their lips an absolutely enthralling and intoxicating sight to behold.

"Violet?"

Starting at the sound of Ives' voice calling her name in question, she darted her gaze into the study, touching on him, and then Cassius. She must look so foolish, standing with her arm outstretched, her fist hovering close to the door, but frozen there, just before making contact with the wooden surface.

"Oh," she said, collecting herself as she cleared her throat in an awkward fashion. "Um, sorry. I . . . I didn't mean to interrupt."

She didn't bother mentioning that she'd not overheard whatever their discussion might've been; she could already tell from the concern in Ives' eyes that her face had clearly shown she'd been distracted when he'd called her name. Cassius, as well, appeared troubled. She felt it clear it hadn't occured to either of them to think she might've instead been attempting to eavesdrop on their whispered dialogue.

With a shake of her head, the young woman forced herself to continue. "I need to speak with both of you."

In a blink, each of them were out of their seats and crossing the room. "Are you all right?" Cassius asked in the same breath as Ives said, "Has something happened?"

It warmed her to see them both show such unabashed consideration of her . . . and perhaps it made her skin tingle and her belly quiver a bit, but she ignored those secondary responding sensations for fear that saying anything while thinking on them might give away her wildly inappropriate feelings for these men. Though, she quite certain they already knew what was in her heart, all the same.

"No, no," she hurried to answer. "I didn't mean to worry you, I apologize. I just, I don't—don't know how else to say this but to come right out with it."

She was nearly positive a look of something like terror flashed across both their faces when she paused there. Her mahogany eyes widening—did they think she was going to leave? Though she couldn't imagine why they'd look afraid rather than sad, or even angry—she shook her head once more. "It's not . . . I feel as though perhaps we've been looking in the wrong places in this Isabeau matter."

The men exchanged a questioning glance.

"I didn't want to say anything," she went on, dropping her gaze to the floor—she was far too aware of how close they stood, that strange coolness they each emitted on occasion making her feel warmer, somehow. "I thought at first I was imagining it, but it keeps happening, it keeps feeling more potent."

"Oh, for the sake of . . . ." Ives uttered the words under his breath before gripping her hand in his, the hold firm but delicate, reassuring. "Violet? Please, just say it."

Her brows shot up at his show of impatience, slight though it was. She was completely sure even someone as consistently calm and assured-seeming as Lord Ives Hayward, II could become flustered and short of temper, she supposed she'd simply never expected to see any sign of that for herself so directly.

Gathering her wits, she nodded. "Right, sorry. I was afraid to say anything because I didn't want to alarm you, but ever since the day we first realized Isabeau was, well, *here*, I have been feeling as if I'm being lured back there. To the old wing."

Cassius' eyes narrowed. "I don't much like the sound of that. I'm not well versed on the subject of specters—of witches or otherwise—but I can't help but feel, if it *is* her, she might be trying to trick you, for some reason."

Violet met his gaze and then turned her attention on Ives. He clearly shared Cassius' thoughts on this.

Frowning, she offered a shrug. She couldn't disagree with the possibility, but they couldn't know that for certain, either. "Thus far, nothing *actually* bad has happened. Oh, surely I was frightened out of my wits a time or two, but that didn't cause me any true sort of harm. It's been more as though she's . . . I know it sounds like madness on the face of it, but it's felt more as though she's trying to get my attention."

"You want to go back, don't you?"

She nodded in answer to Ives' question. "I think we should all go. If you're with me, you won't worry about something happening to me; I know I'll definitely feel safer. And . . . maybe there's, I don't know for certain, something she wants to show us or wants us to find. Perhaps I'm wrong and imagining it, and we'll find nothing, but please. *Please* let's at least go look."

Violet was perfectly cognizant of precisely how much she was asking of Ives. Perfectly cognizant of how much he hated Isabeau Mercier's memory; cognizant of how uncomfortable he was in the old rooms used by his mother before her death. But she knew they would all feel more peace of mind about any discoveries as to what had become of the Mad Witch if those discoveries were made together.

In a very un-Ives-like fashion, the man scowled while he thought it over. After a moment, and finding himself under the combined, not necessarily patient, scrutiny of Violet and Cassius, his expression softened a little.

Uttering a scoffing breath, he arched a brow and offered Violet his arm. "Well, if you insist. It's hardly as though we should let you go back there unaccompanied."

She glanced at Cassius, who returned her gaze with a smarmy grin. His look echoed something she'd heard him say not long after she'd first come to stay with them. That Ives was likely to do anything she asked of him. To her own credit, she kept her features schooled as she slipped one hand around Ives' elbow, and the other around Cassius'.

Though she'd spoken with notes of bravery and determination, she was a bit terrified to return to that room. The chilled sensation running rampant in her midsection made her grateful for their reassuring presence on either side of her as they made their way through the house—and thank the Lord above for the wide corridors of Winterbury Hall, she thought, only half-facetious, or they'd have had quite the adventurous time attempting to traverse the floor without one of the men slapping himself against the walls.

The levity going on in her head those few moments helped distract her from the other, markedly more unpleasant sensations crawling around inside her as they passed the mouth of the staircase and crossed into the old wing. She would gladly pretend it was simply her imagination running away with her when it felt as though the closer they got to the door of Isabeau's guest suite, the harder it became to breathe. Pretend the shadows weren't somehow deeper and darker in this portion of the dusty old mansion than in the other corridors.

Pretend she didn't feel as though her heart was hammering within her ribcage so fiercely, she feared it might actually stop altogether at any moment.

Sooner than she would've liked, they found themselves before the door. Ives stepped away from her side to push it open and walked in ahead of her. She felt Cassius move from her opposite side to stand slightly behind her, curling his arm protectively around her shoulders as they both heard Ives breathe out a shocked sound.

Turning her head, she met Cassius' half-concerned, half-curious gaze before they followed the other man into the room.

Stepping around Ives to place herself beside him, Violet brought her attention to the portrait of Mad Witch Isabeau Mercier. She forced a gulp down her throat.

One brow arched high on her forehead as she asked, "Is that . . . ? Is she—is she really . . . ?"

"Crying blood?" Cassius' voice came out so low, she barely heard him. "Certainly appears so."

Ives, for his part, seemed too shocked to even attempting forming words.

Seeing the two of them so uncertain had an oddly bolstering effect on Violet. In a blink, her fear was gone, replaced with an odd, simmering anger. Looking from one of them to the other, she determinedly grabbed hold of her skirts and started across the room to stand directly before the portrait.

"Well?" she demanded, baring her teeth a bit as she raised her voice. Honestly, she had no idea what had taken hold of her. An overriding desire to act in protection of Ives and Cassius, perhaps? They both seemed so strong and certain all the time, maybe seeing them each taken aback by this peculiar phenomenon was simply more than she could bear. "I'm here! That's what you wanted, isn't it? Was it so you could put on this little show for me?"

No reaction, though she wasn't wholly sure what she had expected. The lighting in the room to recede, leaving only darkness behind? The warmth to leech from the air? The twisting, un-natural feeling shadows in the corners to deepen and warp further?

She could scarcely hear Ives and Cassius be-hind her, murmuring warnings, still shocked and quite uncertain of what to do. Her gaze, however, was trapped by the mournful countenance of one long-dead witch.

"I am here, Isabeau Mercier! Exactly as you wanted, I'm here, and you *will* tell me what it is you expect of me!"

As if in response to Violet's half-shouted statement, a whining metallic sound rent the air. The noise wrenched Cassius and Ives from their immobilized states, each coming up beside her as all three looked about, searching for the source.

Everything happened fast, then.

The enormous painting slipped from its hooks, its heavy gilt frame crashing to the floor with a jarring thud that seemed to shake the entire room and sent up whirling plumes of dust to cloud the air. Ives circled in front of Violet, shielding her from the fall as Cassius clasped his hands in front of her and turned with her in his arms, putting his back to the entire mess.

After a few seconds of deafening silence, Ives looked up, waving his hand before his face in an attempt to clear away some of the floating dust. "Are you two all right?"

"Of course," Cassius answered, coughing as he moved Violet away from him while still keeping a hold of her, just enough to give her a cursory once-over for any injuries. "I think we're all simply shaken up."

"That can't be a coincidence," she said, meeting his gaze and then, squinting in the dust, looking at Ives. "The portrait falls only now? It's been hanging up there for decades yet its hold only gives way *now*? After what we just saw?"

Ives and Cassius shared a glance before all three of them turned to look at the portrait, once more.

"I don't believe it. We *all* saw it, right?" Though neither of them said a word, Violet could sense them nodding in reply as they all stared at the painted face of Isabeau Mercier.

The painted face that showed no sign of blood . . . no sign of *anything*. Just the Mad Witch's unblemished skin and deep, impossibly dark eyes staring back at them.

Chapter Thirteen

Secrets Unfolding

C assius and Violet watched, wary, as Ives approached the mysteriously-fallen portrait. With a tentative hand he reached out, trailing the tips of his fingers over Isabeau's cheeks.

Frowning, his pulled back his arm, brushing the pad of his thumb across his fingertips. "Completely dry."

It was on Violet's lips to suggest the spirit was attempting to get some message across, but no sooner had she thought the words than had Cassius begun to speak. "I don't think scaring us was her intent. Nor harming us—if she could do this, she could've just as easily flung the damn thing and struck us with it. Perhaps she *is* trying to tell us something. Violet's right. There probably is some clue in this room she wishes us to find."

"Why now, though? She's been here so long. Why has she not made herself known before *now*?"

Violet pursed her lips, clasping her fidgeting fingers before her as she answered Ives' question, supplying the reason she'd already considered. "Possibly because she didn't feel she could connect with anyone who wasn't woman?"

"Given what was said of the relationship between Isabeau and Beryl, *and* whatever role your father played in her disappearance? That would seem to make sense," Cassius agreed, shrugging.

Ives didn't appear particularly pleased about any of this, less so that it would mean spending even more time in the Mad Witch's quarters, but he nodded. "That *would* seem to make sense, yes. All right," he conceded whilst breathing out a heavy sigh full of resignation. "Let's look about then, shall we?"

Nodding, they—by unspoken mutual agreement—all took separate sections of the suite. Ives began by sorting through the writing desk by the window, Cassius with the wardrobe, and Violet sifting through the trunk at the foot of the bed.

"Is it strange that your father never disposed of Isabeau's things?" Violet hadn't really meant to voice the question, but her curiosity had the better of her just now, and the words tumbled from her lips sooner than she could think to stop them.

Ives sighed as he sat back in the desk chair. Cassius paused to listen, curious for that answer, as well.

"Honestly? I don't think so. If—" Ives frowned and shook his head, forcing himself to contemplate the matter. "My father was not a kind man, by any means, but he adored my mother . . . in his way. If *she* had refused to be parted from Isabeau's things, he'd have let her keep them."

There was some strained uncurrent in his tone. She wasn't sure how she understood his full meaning, yet she simply did. His father hadn't cared about Beryl keeping Isabeau's belongings as long as Isabeau, herself, was gone . . . and *he* got to keep Beryl.

Violet swallowed hard, leaving her cognizance unspoken and permitting them to return to their searching. The unsettled sense that Beryl's death might've been a blessing in disguise, as it was perhaps her only means of escaping such an awful husband, lodged itself in Violet's heart.

She turned her face away from their view, pretending she was absorbed in her task. A few minutes of listening to the rustling and gentle rifling sounds from Ives' and Cassius' actions helped her to collect herself. After another minute, and a few steadying breaths, she returned to picking through the trunk's contents.

Even as they looked, taking out items, turning them over, shaking them out, whatever was necessary to determine if something might be hidden amongst the pages of some long-unread book, or within the folds of a garment never to be worn again, she knew something wasn't right. Whatever they searched for was not in so simple a place.

Not anywhere that it might've been easily disposed of—wholly by accident—had anyone simply thought to do away with the things in this room. The only person who might've left a clue behind would've been the one person who hadn't wanted Isabeau gone. Ives' mother . . . she'd have seen to it, then, that whatever had been left behind was something that would *stay.*

Closing the trunk with that notion in mind, Violet turned her head, raking her gaze over the room. Every item in here was disposable, and if anything like what some people might do to rid their home of a nasty memory had transpired—toss everything out in a pile and set it ablaze—it would be gone forever. There were no suspicious moldings along the walls or lining where the walls met the ceiling or floorboards . . . .

Rising to her feet, she glued her gaze to the portrait. Violet kept her attention fixed on Isabeau's dark, heavy-lidded eyes as she crossed the room. Though neither man searching the quarters said anything, she was certain she could feel them watching her, wondering what she might be thinking.

Upon reaching the portrait, she ran the tip of her finger along the inner edge of the gilt frame, looking for any loose seam in the canvas. Surely, yes, this would've been burnt up with everything else had the furnishings been done away with in a pyre, but perhaps it was some clue in the painting, itself? Something that would be revealed had the canvas begun to burn?

Yet, she found nothing amiss there.

Frowning, she looked to Cassius and Ives. The portrait as far too large for her to move on her own. "Help me with this," she said, her tone making clear that this was not a request.

Propriety be damned, she *would* get to the bottom of this!

Though they appeared a touch confused, both of them nodded and came to assist her. Ives and Cassius each grabbed hold of one side of the frame and moved it away from the wall. Rather than simply holding it there, however—if their hands were full, they could not readily respond if this were a trick, after all, and the specter did take some violent action—they laid the painting flat against the floor.

"Thank you." She just about breathed the words in a somewhat distracted manner, her gaze once more on the portrait ... or, in this case, on the back of the portrait's frame.

Much like Isabeau's face after the blood tears had vanished, the back was perfectly unblemished. Violet heaved a sigh. She was so sure there might be something there.

Having had enough of this foolishness, but knowing they could not turn their backs on this matter, either, Ives vented his frustration in a way he understood Violet might not be prepared to see from him, yet. But he supposed it was best she learn now that he was not always gentle.

She jumped, her palm flying up to press over her heart at the sound of Ives' fist smashing into the back of the frame. From the corner of her eye, she could see Cassius wince and shake his head, though she could not know if his reaction to Ives putting his fist through the bloody thing was because he thought it a bad idea, or because he was imagining the impact didn't quite tickle.

Violet shook her head, as well. Forcing a gulp down her throat as she took a step closer, watching over Ives' shoulder. When he pulled back his fist and used the hole he'd made to grip his fingers into the backing, she asked, "D' you really think that wise?"

His shoulders moving in a long, silent exhalation, he glanced up at her as he started to break away the pieces. "Violet, my darling, I don't imagine I'll be keeping this in the house once we've put her to rest, so I'm certain she won't mind."

Cassius came to stand beside Violet, folding his arms across his chest and arching a brow. "You're going to give yourself a nasty splinter."

"And then one of you will simply have to play nursemaid and remove it."

His lips tugging to one side, Cassius turned his head to catch Violet's gaze. "That'll be your department."

Despite the gravity of the matter, his quip brought a snicker out of her.

She tried to be patient as Ives just about tore the back of the frame to smithereens—which, by some miracle, didn't manage to give him a single splinter. She did fret that the clue could very well have been *in* the frame, itself, but as he tossed large fragments of the shattered wood panel aside, she glimpsed nothing on their surface.

After the last jagged piece was yanked free and tossed aside, the three found themselves staring at the glaringly blank back of the canvas. Ives was shaking out his hands and flexing his fingers, Cassius' brows inched up his forehead as he pursed his lips, and Violet simply gaped at the untouched fabric.

Ives turned to face her, his mouth open to comment on the fruitlessness of their search, but the words died on his lips. Violet's eyes had taken on a glassy sheen and her features had gone slack. Alarmed by Ives' expression, Cassius pinned his attention on her, as well.

"What ... ?"

She didn't seem to hear him, nor even notice their aghast looks. Instead, she moved away from them. Her steps were plodding and her body moved in an odd, jerking fashion, like a marionette that's puppeteer did not quite have the technique mastered.

Following at a wary distance—yet close enough to stop her if she appeared about to do something dangerous—they found that they were crossing the floor to stand before the writing desk. Violet opened a drawer, not even having to search for which was the correct one, and pulled out a fountain pen and a sheet of aged stationary. Setting the pen to the page, however, the tip made the most unpleasant scratching sound as it scraped, blank, across the surface.

"Dried up," she whispered, her voice utterly empty.

Her next action had both men rushing the few steps to stop her. They moved in the blink of an eye, but so had she—impossibly fast, it seemed —jabbing the fountain pen's sharp point into the tip of her finger.

The young woman did not even flinch.

Turning back to the sheet of paper as though nothing at all had just transpired, she used the blood—dabbing the pen's point back into the open wound once or twice whilst she went, as blood in so limited a quantity did not serve as suitable substitute for ink—to jot down something.

Nodding to no one at all, she set the pen aside, next to the page.

Violet blinked, giving herself a shake. "Ow! What on earth?" She immediately looked to her injured hand, surprised to see the blood dripping from her finger.

Both Ives and Cassius stared at the wound, appearing to be as much in a state of shock as she.

"*What* just happened?" she asked, even as Ives took her hand in his own, examining the injury.

Cassius pulled himself from his stupor and reached around her, picking up the page. "You wrote this. I suspect Isabeau didn't much like that her pen was out of ink."

Scowling, Violet looked back at the upsidedown portrait over her shoulder. "I *really* don't like you." A pleasant sensation drew her attention back to the men before her.

Ives had the tip of her bleeding finger in his mouth.

For a quick, delicious moment, she was remembering those dreams. Those dreams of sinful acts and blood on lips . . . .

She could feel a flush overtake her as she watched him.

Allowing her finger to slip free after having swept along the torn skin with the tip of his tongue, he collected himself. "My apologies if I caught you off-guard. I think I lost my head a little when I saw you'd injured yourself."

Nodding, she swallowed hard. Then she noticed Cassius, watching Ives as well, but his expression was something that bordered on anger, the page on which she'd written Isabeau's message clutched in his hand, unread.

Had the intimacy of the gesture upset him? Or, perhaps, made him feel left out?

Finding herself driven to quell Cassius' simmering temper, she held her wounded finger up to his lips in offering. His attention shot from Ives' face to hers. There was something in his blue eyes... she dared think the word *mesmerized* about the expression, as he leaned his mouth a bit closer, allowing her the chance to change her mind and pull away.

When she held perfectly still—seeming a bit breathless, in fact, as she waited—he clasped his hand around hers. Closing his eyes, he guided her finger between his lips. Once again, she could feel a flood of warmth across her body, the heated skin tingling a bit, as he nipped and suckled playfully at the wound a moment.

He extracted her finger, keeping her hand in his as he opened his eyes again and met her gaze. For a few heartbeats, she was sure no one in the room so much as drew a breath.

Giving herself a shake, she tore her attention from Cassius to look over at Ives. "Oh," she started, seeming to remember the issue of their differing stations—of her post as their employee —then. "I'm so sorry."

They both seemed mystified by her abrupt apology. "Sorry for what?" Ives asked.

"For being so incredibly forward!" Her widened eyes made it clear she thought he was mad to not know why she would feel words of contrition were in order. "That, just now, was *quite* inappropriate of me!"

Ives sighed, shaking his head, and Cassius had yet to relinquish his hold on her hand. "Appropriate or inappropriate is a matter of perspective. I noticed you raise no such fuss when I address you with a term of endearment.'"

"Nor when I get perhaps a bit too close," Cassius tacked on, feigning a tone of utter innocence.

Oh, for pity's sake! There went the warmth flooding her again as she looked from one of them to the other, and back. Were they saying they didn't believe what was going on here between them all was inappropriate? *Or* that the appropriateness of the situation was a matter to be judged by those outside these walls—those who were not here, not involved, and had no say in what went on within Winterbury Hall—and not something with which they should concern themselves?

Despite how she wished it could be that simple, Violet found herself tempted to ask them to elaborate, so she could know for certain what they meant. Instead, for the sake of her own current peace of mind, she opted to get them back on point.

Clearing her throat, she nodded toward the forgotten page of bloodied stationary in Cassius' free hand. "What did I write?"

"Oh, of course." Cassius relinquished his grip on her fingers. A sheepish grin curved his lips, and Ives' equally abashed chuckle sounded on the other side of her.

Turning his attention to her looping, crimson script, Cassius' bright expression dimmed. Looking at Violet and then Ives, he read aloud, "*I am where I was.*"

The three exchanged confused glances as they tried to puzzle out the meaning. *Her* meaning. Isabeau .... Where she *was* ....

Violet's gaze shot to the portrait on the floor, and then to the wall against which it had hung for so very many years. Ice prickled along her skin, down her spine, and unreasonable tears clogged her throat as she realized were Isabeau Mercier *was* .... Where she had been all this time.

The reason Ives' father had left this room and everything it contained untouched even after Beryl had died. The reason no one has been permitted to set foot in this entire wing of the third-floor.

Like something out of a terrible Medieval tragedy. Violet's stomach churned, acidic and cold, with her understanding.

"My God, Ives .... I—I think she's buried in the wall!"

Chapter Fourteen

Vindication

Violet paced the corridor, her arms crossed and one hand pressed to her mouth. She winced with every strike of tools hitting plaster, her shoulders hunching with maddening frequency to match.

Ives had initially thought to temporarily hire on some workers from the nearby towns and villages, but just as quickly realized how foolish that notion was. After his recent missives to authorities about any records pertaining to Isabeau after her disappearance from the estate, there would be *no* keeping it under wraps if any of the workmen saw what they suspected might be behind the wall they sought to open.

No keeping the scandal of his father having murdered a woman and walled up her corpse from becoming local news and the source of filthy idle gossip.

She could feel Cassius' gaze following her rushed, looping strides. Ives had insisted he didn't want her or the other man anywhere near the debris that would get into the air with the destruction of that wall. There was such a heartfelt look in Ives' eyes as he'd pleaded with Cassius to stay away and keep her company out here whilst he dragged poor, subdued Gilbert—with all the workman's tools he could carry—in to assist in his efforts.

Violet knew it was an odd thing to take away from the situation, but bearing this terrible secret with them made her feel as though the three of them had grown closer, still.

Pursing his lips and looking about, Cassius offered, "I know this is . . . awful, but in a way, it sort of feels good, too, doesn't it?"

She halted and whipped up her head to pin her attention on his face. "What are you talking about? What about this horrific scenario could *possibly* feel good?"

With a sigh, he crossed the floor to stand before her. He wrapped his hands delicately around her upper arms as he held her gaze. "I don't mean it in some appalling fashion, Violet. I don't even mean *good*, really, more like . . . vindicating."

She only frowned in response, waiting for him to elaborate. It must be her imagination that just now his touch through the sleeves of her dress felt just a bit warmer than it hard earlier when he'd clasped her hand in his and taken her bleeding finger into his mouth. The notice, alone, had her forcing her mind to ignore the heady sensations that wracked her with that recollection.

"No matter what Ives or I said, you must've still wondered if perhaps you weren't mad, after all, seeing the things you have since coming here?" He shrugged, an impossibly gentle light filling his typically mischievous blue eyes. "You could've written off anything we've done as merely acting on information we'd already had, but that we had simply not considered doing anything about —that we didn't believe there was anything that *could* be done about it—until now. That everything this morning happened with us right there beside you, that you have *proof* there was something to what you'd experienced must be quite the vindicating thing."

"Oh." Violet smiled a bit, nodding. "Yes, I suppose it is. This is just such a terrible situation, I'm bound to think the worst of everything anyone might say about it."

"Perhaps we should go downstairs, or to the gardens, hmm? So you don't have to listen to this racket?"

She crossed her arms, lifting her hands to rest her fingers over his. "The thought is appreciated, but I feel as though I have to be here. I mean, I was the one she reached out to. I know her story is that she did this horrible thing to Ives' mother, but I can't help how I feel. In a strange way, I owe it to her to see this through. To be sure we've found her and that we can lay her to rest."

For a moment he watched her, his expression entirely blank.

Her brows pinched together. "What?"

Cassius visibly forced a gulp down his throat before he could bring himself to speak. His gaze searched hers as he said, "Your compassion... it's a truly remarkable trait. It's one of the things I adore about you."

She was helpless in that moment, enraptured by the way he was looking at her. The sounds of metal striking stone from within the room strangely muffled by how Cassius Vaughn had her attention so wholly captured right now.

"You *adore* things about me?"

"So very many." Oh, his nearly-whispering voice had a breathless edge to it that caused her entire body to warm pleasantly. Seeming caught up, he tacked on, "You do know there is *nothing* on this earth we would not do for you, don't you?"

Somehow, that Ives was on his mind even in this private moment, even as her gaze flicked over his face and he leaned closer, was a wonderful thing to her. Wasn't that strange? Or, at least, shouldn't she think it was? But no. In some bizarre way, she couldn't find it strange. It seemed . . . it *felt* right. Cassius and Ives were linked in a way that made them inextricable from one another in her mind.

One simply did not exist for her without the other.

"Yes," she said, nodding, adoring the sweet tingling sensation of his breath dancing across her lips. "I believe I'm really starting to understand that that's true."

Cassius' mouth covered hers in gentle caress as her eyes drifted closed. No him without Ives, no Ives without him. And Lord help her that she loved them both so much, her heart ached for trying to hold it all.

Just as his hands slid down from where he'd held her, trailing along her sides to loop his arms around her waist, the noise stopped.

Violet pulled back, only enough to meet Cassius' gaze. For a few heartbeats, they merely stared at one another in the silence.

Gilbert's mousy squeak of a voice, trembling a little, interrupted just then from within the room. "Oh, my dear Lord . . . ." His tone made it easy to picture the slip of a man crossing himself as he'd spoken.

Their eyes shot wide and before Cassius could think to stop her, Violet slipped from his arms and ran through the door. Aware this could be a *very* bad thing, Cassius was only a step behind her as she came to a gasping halt in the middle of the floor.

Gilbert looked positively green. Ives' features were pinched in a wholly apologetic look as he turned his attention to Violet. And there, staring back at the room from empty eyes sockets within the hole they'd carved out in the wall, was the half-skeletal face of Isabeau Mercier.

Violet covered her mouth with her hands, reflexively pivoting away from the gruesome image to bury her face in the hollow of Cassius' shoulder. She couldn't even feel the way his arms wrapped around her in equal efforts of comfort and protection. The pictures beating at her brain were too much to focus on anything else, even as she tried to push them away. Isabeau's long, tumbling mass of dark hair was still attached . . . her once plump, olive skin now sallow and withered flesh clinging to bone as though it had been fighting to remain there all these years, waiting to be seen.

There was some sick twisting in Violet's gut, making her wonder if that's where the specter's energy had gone all this time between Isabeau's murder and *her* arrival here. If perhaps, somehow, the ghost of the Mad Witch had sought to preserve her body as much as possible so that if ever the corpse were discovered, there would be precious little room to question its identity.

"Take her outside, Cassius. I'd rather her not have to witness anything more than this," Ives said through clenched teeth. As Cassius started to lead Violet back toward the door, Ives told Gilbert, "Fetch Father Callahan, Saint Catherine's Church. He's ... an old friend of the family. He can perform a proper funeral service to put her to rest *and* keep things quiet."

"Wait!" Violet called that single word over her shoulder. She didn't turn back, didn't dare cast her gaze upon Isabeau's marred visage again, keeping her attention fixed on the empty corridor before her, Cassius' guiding arm around her waist.

"Violet," Ives started, his tone gentle, but with an edge of impatience to it, "it's best if this is all handled quickly. My feelings about her past aside, she's been in a state of unrest long enough."

"Oh, I'm not denying that, of course, but ...." Swallowing hard, she lifted her hand to shield her eyes and turned, facing into the room. "According to the stories, Isabeau may have had a different, um, belief system than any to which *we* are accustomed. That's to say ... she might not be Christian, at all. As such, Christian burial rites might *not* put her to rest. They might only antagonize her further."

"Bloody hell, that hadn't even occurred to me," Ives said, a weary sigh spilling out with the words. "Unfortunately, without any further information about her, I'm uncertain how to proceed otherwise."

"She was a spiritualist, wasn't she? A rumored 'witch'?"

Cassius uttered a soft, breathy sound. "I see what you're getting at."

Violet met his gaze, but didn't drop the hand that was blocking the ghastly sight from her view. She nodded, noting his fairly grim expression. Grim *and* concerned, and she didn't blame him. When these things were nothing but showy hokum, there was no harm to them—except perhaps that some bereaved loved one's coin purse got a bit lighter. But when an actual specter, capable and unafraid of reaching out to the living, was on hand?

"What are you two going on about?" Ives asked, clearly not comprehending Violet's meaning.

Again, she nodded to Cassius. Tearing his gaze from hers, he looked across the room to Ives. "She's talking about conducting a séance."

Violet couldn't see the way squirrely little Gilbert's brows pinched together, his mouth dropping into a tiny, shocked *O* as he looked to his employer, as well, awaiting the lord's reply. Cassius would've found the butler's expression hilarious if not for the grave matter . . . well, that and the half-decomposed body staring back at them all.

"All right. I don't like the idea very much, but you've a point. This woman's been done enough injustice, I will not add to her miseries." Ives heaved a weighted sigh, raking his fingers through his thick brown curls. "However, I'm not certain how to proceed with such a thing."

It was difficult to focus on what Isabeau might—or might not, who knew if the story was even true, anymore—have done to his mother. Not after seeing what had become of her.

"I've attended a few séances. Some of Uncle Hugh's society chums are quite enamored with Spiritualism. I think I can manage." Though, Violet was half-certain she'd only retained *any* of it because the absurdity of such things had a way of drawing one's attention, no matter the attendee's reluctance to believe. She shrugged, rushing on before anyone could voice a protest. "Isabeau has already made herself known to me several times. It won't be difficult for me to make contact with her, I'm sure."

"That surety is what concerns us," Ives said, his tone stern. "We are well aware she will probably respond readily to any attempt you make to summon her. But she took control of you once, already, when no such attempt was even being made, caused you to injure yourself—"

"You know that wasn't her intent!"

"Nevertheless, if that is the power she wields over you when you've not given her providence to speak to or through you, I daresay *inviting* her to do so could have disastrous implications. For all we know, she could attempt to possess you!"

"Hence why you will be with me the entire time, both of you. If anything at all goes wrong— even a little bit—you interrupt the session. That's all it takes." Her tone was somewhere between reasonable and pleading. "The interruption will break our connection. We only need her here long enough to answer the question of how she would like us to handle her remains. We thank her, bid her farewell, end the session, and then follow her request."

"It's terrifying how you make it sound like a small thing."

She cut an unhappy look at Cassius, her lips pursed. "Well, it is. Or, at least, it should be. And it is the least anyone can do for a person who's been trapped adrift between life and death for so many years."

Violet could hear the sound of Ives slapping his hand against his face. "All right, all right," he said. "You make me feel any lower and Gilbert'll have to scrape me off the floorboards. You two go on, leave Gilbert and me to get her out, and put her someplace more . . . suitable?" Oh, it had been rough to find a proper word there, but he could hardly leave the poor woman propped up right within a hollowed-out bedroom wall!

"Right. That'll be plenty of time to have the séance this evening, after sundown."

Cassius and Ives shared a look, each nodding reluctantly. "Where?" they asked in the same breath.

Exhaling as she thought it over, she recalled something one of the so-called mediums had said during the seance at Uncle's most recent party

—but then the medium, the bubbly and seemingly perfect Dorothea Wolstone, was more likely memorable on account of how unlikely of person she seemed for such a thing than anything outstanding she'd done in contacting the spirit realm. "It should, if available, be done in a space to which the deceased had some connection in life. So *here.* Right here in this room." She swallowed hard, crinkling the bridge of her nose. "And we keep the body here, too."

Cassius and Ives both protested, but she held up a silencing hand—shocked when they both simmered down instantly in response. "Not in the wall, but in here. Having a personal object from the person is best, however, I don't feel like anything we've found in this room was something that could be considered deeply personal. She might have those sort of things *on* her—a ring that was a family heirloom, or a necklace she cherished since childhood—and it wouldn't feel right to remove those from her for our own purposes. Therefore, as odious a thought as it is, having her here would be the best way to ensure a connection is made."

"If you're going to insist, so be it." Ives shook his head, sighing yet again. "For now, however, leave while we at least remove her from the wall."

Violet nodded, her limbs somewhat numb as she allowed Cassius to lead her out. *What* had she just agreed to do? Not only agreed to, but been the one to suggest!

Dear God, she might be going mad after all!

Chapter Fifteen

Truth Will Out

Violet stared at the table Gilbert had set in the center of Isabeau's room. As she'd instructed, it was a simple table of modest size, a single unlit candle set in the middle. To one side he'd placed a small vesuvian box, to the other —as Isabeau had chosen to communicate through written word previously—some sheets of the ghost's favored stationary and a *working* fountain pen. Violet's bandaged finger still smarted from the unfortunate incident with the dried up implement earlier.

At present, the only illumination in the

room was the lantern Ives held high. Upon her lighting of that candle, the lantern would be extinguished, plunging the room into as complete a darkness as possible. Isabeau had been laid upon the bed, wrapped securely in a white sheet. There seemed some cruel, twisted mockery, unintended though it had been, in settling her so peacefully, as though she were only at rest. Shrouded as the corpse was, it was simple to imagine that was merely a slumbering, perfectly alive person there in the shadows.

Gilbert, seeming rather more skittish than usual in regard to the evening's proceedings, had been permitted to retire to his quarters for the night after preparing the room. She could sense Ives and Cassius' wary gazes on her as she stepped from the space where the three of them had been clustered after the butler's departure, just inside the door.

They had to get this started some time, and she was the focal point for Isabeau's messages. It was a cold, mechanical way to think on the matter, but she held no illusions about the depth of her significance—she was merely part of a relay system without which the specter's words might never be known to the living.

She turned to look back at them. "C'mon," she said, offering an encouraging smile that she only wished she could feel was confident in the slightest. "I need you two close. Just in case."

"Of course," Ives answered with a nod whilst

he crossed the room to follow her. Cassius was silent, but also moved at her behest, all the same.

As they approached the table, Violet indicated each of them to stand on either side of the lone chair. She wanted them near enough that they could interfere if needed, yet just far enough away that Isabeau would not feel uncomfortable if she truly did have an issue communicating directly with men.

Squaring her shoulders, Violet tried to bolster her nerves, reminding herself of the good this would do—the peace it would bring, not only to one restless specter, but to the house, itself. No more whispers, no more darkened corridors hosting even darker silhouttes of people long-passed. She drew in a rattling breath and forced it back out before withdrawing the chair and seating herself.

She flexed her fingers a few times, trying to lessen some of the sudden nervous energy in her hands. "All right," she said in a whisper, her voice low as she reminded Ives once more, "when the candle is lit, turn down the lantern."

"I've not forgotten, Violet."

The young woman nodded, focusing as well as she could on her breathing. *In . . . out . . . .* She reached for the box and withdrew a match. *In . . . out . . . .* Striking the match, that sound of friction seemed deafening in the otherwise silent room. *In . . . out . . . .* Her hand trembled a little as she lifted the match to the wick.

In . . . out . . . .

The wick caught, and Ives extinguished the brighter illumination of the lantern. There was a faint metal clatter as he set it aside that seemed to ring in Violet's ears.

In ... out ....

"I call to the spirit of Isabeau Mercier," she said, her voice louder than she'd ever imagined she'd be able to make it with her nerves as wracked as they were just now. Her gaze fixed on the standing flame of that single candle, she forced herself to continue, "I implore you, make your presence known to me that I might help you find peace."

That single lick of fire moved. Dancing on its wick as the wax began to drip along the tapered length of the candle, Violet felt her breath catch in her throat. So dazzled by the spot of flickering brightness, she thought perhaps she imagined she was seeing things within.

Faces.

Movements.

The moment the luster had faded from Isabeau's dark eyes.

The terror of realizing the breath she'd just drawn was her last.

The odd, dull listlessness that draped her senses like a fog.

Violet tried to remain focused, but she wasn't even sure if what she asked next was in her head or spoken aloud as she said, "Please, Isabeau. You've languished long enough. Answer this *one* question I put to you: what would you have us do with your remains so that you might pass on from this place?"

She wasn't certain of any answer. For some time . . . mere heartbeats, full minutes, she couldn't keep account . . . she lost all cognizance of her surroundings. There was only the flame before her, only the low, muffled echo of her own words in her mind.

The fear of uncertainty. The question of what she'd done to meet such a brutal end tied Violet's stomach in knots and set an icy chill wrapping her shoulders.

The disorientation of her vision going dim . . . . Of sounds ceasing to make sense to her ears.

And then *nothing*. Complete and utter. Nothingness. Heartbreaking nothingness.

Gone.

All gone.

Beryl.

Light.

Feeling.

Gone.

Abject horror at imagining Beryl fading in the absence of her magic, lost to this wretched illness which medical science claimed did not exist simply because it held no cure.

Loneliness like a living thing that strangled the heart.

Darkness that became eternity.

There could be no light without Beryl, anyway.

Gone.

"Violet!"

She choked down a gasp, her eyes snapping open. The flame had been extinguished and Cassius knelt beside her, his arm curled around her shoulders as Ives saw to relighting the lantern. Her entire frame seemed to tremble in Cassius' protective embrace and she looked to her hands. One palm was pressed to a piece of the stationary, the other grasped the pen. That same looping script from earlier had appeared on the page, yet Violet hadn't the faintest recollection of even picking up the pen, let alone writing anything.

The bothersome sensation of tears pinging the corners of her eyes forced her to blink a few times as she tipped her head to one side, letting Cassius press his cheek against the top of her head. She angled her gaze toward Ives as he knelt on her other side.

"I don't understand, what happened? Why did you end it? Did she try to hurt me, after all?"

She was aware of the men exchanging a glance before Ives answered. "We didn't end it. *She* did. You fell into a trance so fast it—well, frankly, it terrified us—but then, after you asked her to come, you picked up the pen and started writing. Yet, when you'd finished writing, you wouldn't wake. And following that ... you screamed."

"I did?"

Ives nodded as Cassius snickered. "Almost startled me into needing a new pair of trousers."

Violet couldn't help but laugh in return at the younger man's typically inappropriate response.

"But yes, you screamed," Ives reiterated, his tone not reflecting their moment of levity. "It was then that the candle simply went out."

"I was so caught up in what she was showing me." It frightened Violet a little that she'd been so very susceptible to such a thing that the ghost, herself, had been the one to break the connection.

"I saw . . . *felt* the moment she died, I think. She was dying, still, when her put her in the wall."

Ives' already fair skin drained of color entirely and Cassius shivered in revulsion at her side.

"I don't think finding her would have saved her life. She was . . . *going*. The light in her eyes had left . . . there was nothing anyone could've done, even if they'd kept her from being hidden away." She reached out, clasping both of her hands around Ives' empty one, her vision misty and her voice catching a little. "Even in that moment, your mother was on her mind. I don't think she was as wicked as the stories held, Ives. I believe Isabeau truly *did* love her."

She again blinked away the sensation of tears prickling in her eyes as she added cautiously, "I think she showed me that it was her magic that was keeping your mother's illness at bay. That was why she became so ill whenever Isabeau was sent away." Violet swallowed hard. "Her last thoughts weren't of her fear of death, nor the darkness, but of worrying what would become of Beryl without her."

Ives' blue eyes searched Violet's face as his mouth pulled into a grim line, sparing a moment for her observations to sink in. "I have suspected since this . . . macabre little adventure of ours began that my father was the villain in this story. The only say that was ever had about Mother's condition having improved following Isabeau's death was *his*. I had assumed the vilness of his actions limited to what he might've done to make Isabeau disappear." His voice became low and thick as he went on, "But now, I understand it didn't end there. He vilified *her*. Twisted any tell of her in this house to cover—worse, to justify— his crime."

If she didn't know any better, Violet would swear there were unshed tears of his own swimming Ives' eyes, then. Not that such a thing could be held against him; none of this could be easy for him. Nodding, she pulled away from Cassius just enough to sit up properly, but did not extract herself from his hold. She would not share any more of what she'd experienced with them. That would be a secret between her and Isabeau. Nothing helpful to any of them would come from relaying those terrible feelings.

Now that she understood the situation more completely, Violet suspected that if she could've, Isabeau would have stopped her from picking up any of it so directly.

Turning her attention to the sheet of stationary, she motioned for Ives to bring the lantern closer. He set it atop the table, leaning against her other side. She loved the comfort of feeling both of them crowd close around her like this.

"Put me to pyre at the witching hour." Violet swallowed hard, a sad smile curving her lips. "Well, we have a few hours. That's plenty of time to prepare such a thing. We can actually have her put to rest tonight."

"There's more," Cassius pointed out, tapping some smudged ink at the bottom of the page.

Lifting the paper toward the light, she frowned. The words had been smeared a bit by her palm, and it took her a moment to discern the blurred letters.

The moment she did, however, a sheen of ice coated the pit of her stomach. "Oh."

"What is it?"

Violet was afraid to say. She'd not told them anything of this. There'd been too much fear. The dreams had been bad enough, but the . . . . The *monstrous* part of the dreams that she no longer thought so monstrous?

That devilish part that she'd come to think of as being so alluring . . . .

Finding herself unable to answer the question they'd asked in unison, Violet felt tears gather all over again. She didn't know if they were from fright or sadness. "I shouldn't say. This part seems a private message to me from Isabeau."

"I see. If I didn't know any better, I would think she took a liking to you." Ives nodded, closing his hand around Violet's over the secret message. "I'll fetch Gilbert to help with this pyre. I expect you'll wish to be there?"

"Of course. As I said to Cassius earlier, I feel as though I owe it to her to see this through." Pushing back her chair, she stood, clutching the paper to her chest.   It wrenched a heart a bit that they trusted her so completely, they didn't even wonder what Isabeau's private message was. "But I've had a bit of a trying day. I think I'll get some rest before then, if that's all right?"

"Certainly."

Violet was quiet as they led her out into the corridor. Quiet as they walked with her back across the house to her own room. Quiet, but afraid she might let out some telling sound as Ives brushed a kiss across the back of her hand, as Cassius was a bit bolder, dropping a kiss on her cheek, whilst they bid her good evening *if only for a few hours.*

Closing the door between them, she turned and put her back to it. After a handful of shuddering breaths, she crossed the floor to the lantern on her bedside table. The sparse illumination from the moonlight streaming through the window permitted her to see just well enough that she was able to light it, despite her trembling fingers.

Seating herself upon the edge of the mattress, she smoothed out the page against her leg. In the glow of the lantern, she studied the words, once more. Assured, now, that she'd not misread Isabeau's smudged writing, Violet felt another wrenching pain in her chest that outweighed her immediate fear of the message.

Believe the blood.

The pinches . . . the crimson stained lips . . . the twin marks that she glimpsed in her dreams, but were always gone by the light of morning.

But how? She'd seen Ives and Cassius in daylight.

Yet, didn't they always appear paler whilst the sun hung in the sky?

She'd seen them eat food.

But they never commented on the taste, never made sounds of satisfaction when the meal was exceptional. As though . . . as though the act of eating was . . . mechanical for them.

Violet crushed the paper against her heart as her eyes drifted closed.

Their touch was always a bit cool. Except . . . except in the mornings. They seemed to lose some warmth as the day wore on. Just as how Cassius' skin had felt warmer against hers after he'd taken the blood she'd offered him from her wounded finger.

She didn't know what to feel. Didn't know if she could truly believe her own mind, just now. They cared for her, she knew they did, possibly even loved her—adored her, as Cassius had admitted just earlier that very day. And she certainly loved them. So then, how ... ?

How could it be that they were monsters out of some old world myth? Could she pretend they weren't simply because those myths didn't seem to hold against reality?

Violet understood with a staggering, deep-rooted certainty that she'd known for so long, now. It should affect her feelings for them, but it did not. She should be terrified of them, and yet she was not. She *knew* what they were, yet she still could not bring herself to truly believe.

How could Ives Hayward and Cassius Vaughn be *vampires*?

Chapter Sixteen

Sounds in the Night

She'd not slept a wink by the time Ives knocked on her door shortly before midnight. Violet had fretted over what to do. In the end—and at long last, it seemed—she'd relented to logic.

Her trunk was much too heavy for her to lug about easily on her own, so she'd instead nicked a satchel from the servants' quarters and loaded it down with as many of her things as it would hold. She would simply have to leave the rest behind. The overstuffed bag waited for her, secreted away beneath her bed, as she slipped out into the corridor to join him and Cassius, a forced smile plastered across her face.

So badly she wanted to follow her heart and stay, but how could she, knowing what she did now? Tonight, after this, she'd slip away. Oh, sure, fine picture she'd make, lone young woman traipsing along the road to the nearest town in the wee hours of the morning with naught but the clothes on her back and a sack ready to burst over her shoulder. But she wasn't certain what else to do. There was no arranging for a carriage without Ives and Cassius finding out, and her precious logic —which she'd almost entirely ignored whilst she was living here—dictated that she leave as soon, and as inconspicuously, as possible.

When she descended the staircase between them and crossed the ground floor toward the foyer, she tried to quiet the painful, thundering beat of her heart. She listened to them speaking on the oddity of this entire Isabeau situation, overwhelmed for a moment by how much she was going to miss the sounds of their voices. Each glance toward either of their faces pried another ache from her chest at how woundingly cognizant she was that she would long to look into their eyes again after she was gone.

Often.

Very possibly for the rest of her life.

Every gentle touch or fleeting caress of their fingers against hers made her wonder if they could truly be monsters when they treated her like such a treasured thing?

Around the back of the main house, Gilbert had built the up a large bundle of kindling into a rough platform. Isabeau's body lay atop, still shrouded in that white linen; her belongings were gathered neatly into the pile, and the lot of it sprinkled liberally with parafin. This was it. Any and all scraps of Isabeau Mercier's existence in Winterbury Hall. Everything would burn, winds would scatter the ashes over the days that followed. Nothing more to tether her here.

Violet stepped away from Ives and Cassius, taking hold of the lit candle Gilbert held out for her. By some miracle, there was barely a breeze just now.

She waited, swallowing hard as she stared at Isabeau's form. Closing her eyes, Violet whispered a small prayer. Oh, certainly, she thought the witch might not appreciate the thought, but it wasn't even truly a prayer. Violet's muttered words asked simply that Isabeau Mercier be permitted to rest peacefully. That she no longer be disturbed by the torments of her last moments alive.

Checking the timepiece upon her wrist, the candlelight glinted off the face as she counted down the seconds. At 11:59, she stepped directly up before the assemblage of wood and personal effects. Closing her eyes, Violet bowed her head, repeating her small not-really-a-prayer beseechment. Opening them, she looked again.

Drawing a deep breath, she let it out slow as she counted backward from ten.

At last, the hands both pointed to 12. Nodding, she whispered as she pressed the flame into the kindling and waited for it to catch, "Rest well, Isabeau Mercier."

As the fire built, she stepped back. Her attention fixed upon the pyre as the orange-yellow glow consumed the image before her by increments, she felt the moment Ives and Cassius had moved up on either side of her.

They were all silent as they watched the fire.

Violet let her eyes drift close as she felt their cool hands wrap around each of hers. She willed herself to remember the sensation of their skin on hers, to remember the feeling of them stationing themselves so close and so protectively beside her.

Safe under the guise of reacting to all that had happened today, Violet allowed herself to cry.

She wasn't even gone yet, but already she missed them so much she could scarcely breathe.

An hour had passed after returning to her

room by the time she worked up the courage to drag out the satchel from beneath her bed and sling it over her shoulder. But then, it wasn't truly a matter of fear, she recognized that. It was the struggle with herself. Her heart told her these men might be monsters, but they were *her* monsters, and they'd never harm her.

Logic dictated that if she remained with them, harm would come to her, even were in not by their hands or whims.

Lord, did she *hate* logic just now.

And logic felt a bit like madness in this moment. Vampires didn't exist! They *didn't!* But then, neither did witches or ghosts, yet she'd just burned a witch's body at the behest of said witch's own ghost, so what the bloody hell did *she* know?

Violet opened her door and stepped out, pulling it closed as soundlessly as she could behind her. Tears crowded her throat as she turned toward the staircase.

Maybe she should confront them, instead. Rather than simply vanishing into the night, as they'd wondered if Isabeau had before they'd found her. Walking away from them was difficult enough, she wasn't sure she could bear the weight of leaving them behind without a word, as well.

But then, perhaps *she* was mad.

Pivoting on her heel, she instead faced toward the opposite wing, where their rooms were. Yes, she should at least confront them. If they laughed off her suspicions and it turned out she was, in fact, no longer sane—despite Ives' demonstration to the contrary—at least there would be some strange relief there. Oh, certainly, she'd be languishing in an asylum, but she would do so knowing she had imagined all this and fairy tale monsters were only that—the substance of fairy tales.

Dropping the satchel beside the staircase landing, she started back along the corridor. Oh, this was probably a terrible idea. They'd try to convince her to stay. And perhaps she wanted them to . . . .

It was hard enough imagining them saddened and confused by her decision as it was, toss sleep-rumpled on there and she wasn't certain of her decision to confront them about her departure and her reasons, at *all.*

And, then again, she might just be trying to stall her exit from the house. She seemed the very definition of indecisiveness right now.

Reaching Cassius' door—she thought to wake him and then pull him along with her to Ives' room so that she might speak with them both at once—she lifted her hand to knock. Yet, a sound from inside the room halted her, mid-motion.

Licking her lips in an anxious gesture, she gave herself a shake. Preparing to knock once more, she was again stopped by a noise from within. The sort she readily recognized now from those dreams.

Curious in spite of her emotional state, Violet dropped her hand to her side and quietly shifted her skirts so that she could lower to her knees. Leaning near, she reprimanded herself in a seething internal whisper as she peered through the keyhole.

The sight before her caught her breath in her throat. She brought up her free hand to cover her mouth, but couldn't seem to look away.

Ives knelt on the floor beside Cassius' bed, his entire body bared to her eyes. He was curled forward, over the other man's lap. One arm around Cassius' naked hips, Ives' other hand was assisting his mouth as he—

Oh, my Lord! I should not be watching this!

Yet she still could not tear her gaze from the sight. Ives' rhythmic motions, Cassius' head falling back as he gripped his fingers into Ives' hair. She couldn't deny a sweet, flickering warmth that the spectacle sent rippling through her.

"It's not quite enough," Cassius said in near-growling whisper.

Though he uttered what sounded like a chuckle, Ives didn't lift his head from his task. He unwound his arm from Cassius' hips, offering up his wrist.

Clutching his free hand around Ives', Cassius let out an ecstatic sigh. He bared his teeth, the canines easing out into longer, needle-sharp points. She could actually hear the sound of it as he brought Ives' wrist to his lips and bit down.

GERILYN MARIN

That was when a noise she couldn't stifle escaped her.

The denial she'd clung to all this time—even as she'd called them what they were, even as she'd literally packed a bag and plotted an escape—shattered, falling away from her like shards of broken glass. It was true, all along it had been true! All along she'd known on some level, but here it was before her very eyes. Cassius was taking Ives' blood, the way she'd experienced them both doing with her in all those dreams. Dreams that had never been dreams at all, but simply hazy memories she'd hidden from herself.

And she'd drawn a gasp as those realization struck.

The startled sound from outside the door caught both men's attention, and they immediately stopped what they were doing to look in her direction. "Violet?" they said in unison. Ives shot to his feet and started toward the door, grabbing a dressing gown from the end of the bed on his way.

Panic clogging her throat, Violet scrambled off the floor and tore across the corridor, back toward the staircase. She could hear the door opening behind her and Ives' footfalls as he followed.

How she made it down the staircase without tripping over her skirts in her hurry was beyond her. She didn't even have the presence of mind to grab the satchel as she went past. They *knew* she knew, now, and not in some fashion that could be shrugged off and explained away.

She raced across the ground floor, yet somehow Ives managed to get ahead of her, rounding to place himself before the doors as she ran into the foyer. Violet stumbled to a halt, barely keeping her footing. He caught her around the waist and steadied her.

She hadn't ever before thought they'd have harmed her, but after *actually* witnessing proof of what they were . . . ? "Please don't hurt me," she said, her voice spilling out in a trembling whisper as she struggled out of his hold, backpedaling a step.

His brows pinched together, a wounded expression coloring his features as he shook his head. "We would *never!*"

"But I saw it! I *saw* you and him. I—I know the things I dreamed were real, now!" She pressed her hands to the sides of face as she forced herself to go on, bewildered tears welling in her eyes. "You, both of you, you seduced me and took my blood. How is that *not* hurting me?"

"Because it was you who invited us," Cassius' voice rang out from atop the staircase.

Violet tore her attention from Ives and pivoted on her heel to peer back into the depths of the house. Unlike Ives, Cassius had not bothered covering himself at all. Gloriously nude, he stood there staring back at her, his expression strangely open and trusting. What an odd thing to notice in such a moment, she thought.

"Good Lord, man. A dressing gown would've

killed you?" Ives asked in a hissing breath.

Cassius shook his head, a thoughtful frown gracing his lips as he started down the staircase. "There would be little point as she's seen everything, already. Besides, I'll hide *nothing* from her any longer."

All of Violet's proper sensibilities were screaming at her to look away, to blush and act appropriately abashed by Cassius' behavior and . . . wanton nakedness. Yet, she could not seem to tear her gaze away from him. More, she didn't want to, and for more reasons than how painfully beautiful he was.

It seemed madness that she was standing here at all. But then, with the way Ives had moved just moments ago—quicker than should've been possible—to reach the front doors ahead of her, Violet knew she had no hope of outrunning them if she tried to bolt from the house.

Remembering how he'd slipped across the ground floor so fast, there was a sudden, hazy recollection playing before her mind's eye. When the painting of Isabeau had fallen, Ives and Cassius hadn't simply moved quickly to protect her —they'd moved faster than was humanly possible, she simply had not registered the swiftness of their actions at the time, there had been too much going on. When she'd stabbed herself with the pen, they'd been unable to stop her simply because the movement had been so very unexpected and sudden.

They *had* tried to protect her. She supposed the least she could do was give them room to explain this madness. "What do you mean, I invited you? I don't understand," she said, her tone pleading. "I don't feel like I understand *any* of this."

"We'll tell you everything you want to know."

She gave a nod, pouting in a mix of anger and confusion. Gone, now, was her fear. Though, the wild desire to openly stare at Cassius' naked form was rampant and distracting, she forced herself to ignore that for the time being.

"Good, because that's precisely what I want to know. *Everything.*"

Chapter Seventeen

Old Promise, Older Myth

"I'll start at the beginning, then." Cassius took one of her hands between both of his, she could feel the cold of his skin against hers. As all the other times either of them touched her, she found a strange comfort in it, somehow feeling warmer for the mild chill of his flesh. She could sense it as Ives stepped up closer behind her.

"We were as truthful with you as we could manage whilst not divulging our secret." He paused then, exchanging a heartfelt look with Ives over her shoulder. "When I was turned, I *was* sickly. It's . . . it's nothing like the fanciful old stories. Stories that were started *by* vampires, by the way. Made it easier for us to hide if lies about how to find us, how we lived, were given to the world as truth 'if' we even existed, I think was the idea. It isn't some miracle cure, nor do you even truly die. We simply sort of . . . stop. I didn't know strength, I didn't know a lack of feeling. There was no one to see me through it. I think my maker believed those stories, too, because I was left for dead. I languished as my body tried to heal itself, yet couldn't die. And Ives was the first kind soul I'd met in, oh, it must've been fifty years I'd been a vampire by then?"

"I didn't know what Cassius was, not at first," Ives continued the story, resting his hands gently around her waist, as though holding her whilst they had *this* discussion was the most natural thing in the world. "I knew he needed help, that was enough for me. I discovered what he was entirely by accident. And, I knew after the story of what had happened with my mother and Isabeau, my father'd have killed Cassius if he suspected another 'monster' had come to harm what was left of his family, so I secreted him away in this house. And, as my mother had . . . I love men *and* women, equally, another thing I knew he would not understand. As I already told you, my father was advanced in age when I was born, so it was not long we had to wait before he passed naturally and we no longer had to hide."

"Funny enough, Isabeau was not the only

witch in this story, but we'll get to that." Cassius lifted her hand, still clasped between both of his, to brush his lips against the tips of her fingers. "It's been just a decade shy of a hundred years since Ives' father passed. I believe you noted how strange it was that everything in the old wing seemed so much longer unused than a mere twenty-some-odd years ago, hmm?"

Violet nodded, the motion a bit numb as she remembered thinking exactly that, but now, too, did other things she'd not readily paid attention to make sense. Isabeau's portrait was rendered in a style that had fallen out of favor early in the Georgian era. So, too, had her wardrobe as well as the very dress and refinements that had still been on her when they'd discovered her body been of Georgian style, rather than Victorian. The outdated attire of the fine gentlmen in those aged portraits now made perfect sense, as she undertood they'd not been outdated at all, but that she'd simply been misled about *when* things had taken place.

Had her drive to disbelieve been so strong that she'd forced herself not to notice these things?

Cassius went on, using his hands on hers to press her palm over his heart, letting her feel the dull, impossibly slow thudding of it beneath his cool skin. "We were not wholly dishonest about the necessity of your tutoring skills, nor my lack of formal education. I was sickly for so long. Ives doted on me, took care of me entirely, I was bed-ridden for years. I simply didn't have the strength for much of anything. Ives had me turn him so that he could stay by my side. He would go so far as to lure vagabonds to the house for me."

Her brow furrowed, thoroughly engrossed in Cassius' story in spite of herself. "Did you kill them?"

Cassius shook his head. "There was little need for that, and we—Ives and I—have been bound from killing for sustenance. Besides, they were happy to exchange a bit of their blood for a hot meal and a handful of crowns for the road, no questions asked. It kept my condition from worsening, but it wasn't enough to truly sustain me."

"What changed?" Her voice sounded hollow, foreign to her own ears.

"You."

Violet had to force herself to ignore the vaguely awestruck look that had overtaken his features as he said that one little word. "What?" She was aware of Ives resting his chin atop her head. Perhaps it was right, somehow, that she pictured him closing his eyes in a serene expression as he listened to his lover's telling of their story.

"After Ives discovered what I was, he insisted on finding a way to cure my affliction. So, he located a witch. A true witch, like Isabeau had been. Yet, after bringing her here to see me for herself, she . . . took pity on us, despite that she could do nothing to help, and shared a secret that could change the very existence of those like me, changed against their will—those like Ives, changed out of love at their own request. But there was a price."

"You could never kill anyone?"

The corners of Cassius' mouth plucked upward in a bitter mockery of a smile as he nodded. "She didn't know that I'd not fed to the point of death, but she did understand it's not easy for our kind to control ourselves when we feed, either. The only reason I'd not killed anyone, yet, had been because I simply lacked the strength. I swore that if I ever healed, I would try not to. And Ives, intent on remaining with me, also swore that never would he, either. It is a promise we've kept for a century."

Violet had an odd feeling there was some part of her that already knew the next bit of the story, but still she asked—she needed to actually hear it. She needed the spoken words to pull the mysteriously begotten knowledge from the recesses of her mind. "What was the witch's secret?"

"We weren't even certain if it was true, but we were willing to believe it could be. Cassius didn't want to die, and I didn't want to lose him. He might not have been able to succumb to his illness, but with every day that passed of him in such constant misery, I feared he might eventually be tempted to take his own life," Ives said, the faintest hint of tears edging his whispered voice. "Long ago, a pair not unlike ourselves made a plea. Call it God, the Universe, the Powers That Be, but according to the witch, *something* answered. Something that, like her, took pity on them. Whatever that power was, it pledged that there would be a way for monsters such as we, who went through the torment of abstaining from their brutal natures. That way came in the form of the *Sanguinem Aeterna.*"

"Doesn't . . . ?" She swallowed hard, her gaze locked on Cassius' even as she shook her head beneath the weight of Ives' chin. "Doesn't that mean something like eternal blood?"

Cassius nodded, once more lifting Violet's hand to kiss the tips of her fingers. "There came to be a bloodline, mixed in amongst humanity, of those who could exist along with us, remaining by our side for eternity. But only those who kept to the promise would be led to finding such people. Their blood is . . . magical, in a sense. It constantly replenishes. *But* it's not as simple as someone merely taking their blood."

"Forgive me," Ives said, slipping his arms around her to hold her in a gentle embrace against him. "I knew it was you from the time you scraped your knee the day we'd first met. I managed to salvage a bit of your blood and I brought it home to Cassius. The moment it touched his lips, his health improved. It was a miracle, and then we *knew.*"

"I'm one of these people?" This couldn't be true. Witches, ghosts, vampires? Oh, sure. Those she knew now were all real, but humans with unending blood? *That* seemed a bit much, even with the nagging feeling in the pit of her stomach that it was true. Surely, she'd always been a fast healer, but she'd never attributed that to, well, anything. Never really thought about it before, at all.

Frowning she turned her attention to her free hand. Lifting it before her eyes, she stared at the bandage winding her finger for a moment. She knew that if she removed it right now, the split in her skin from Isabeau's fountain pen would be healed.

"It was by sheer luck that you were a ward of the Sinnet family. Hugh's grandfather had a nasty problem. The old sod was deeply in debt and in danger of losing everything his family had. Their financial holdings, their lands, their social standing. They were literally on the verge of ending up in a debtors prison, utterly disgraced and penniless. But he was one of the few people who'd realized what we are. He tried to blackmail us into giving him money to repay his debts. I did more than that. I made it so it was as though he'd never spent even a hay penny in his entire life. When he realized how generous we'd been when we—being *monsters*, of course—could've just as easily killed him, he swore his family to repay that excess. One favor, whatever we might ask of them when the time came to call upon their service."

"So you arranged for Uncle Hugh to send me here?" That was why he wouldn't see her off, why he was hung on words of her continued safety and happiness, according to Fletcher's letters. Uncle Hugh felt guilty for what he'd done, but he likely assumed he was protecting Fletcher. The sense that she'd never truly been as important to the family as a blood-relation had always weighed on her, but to actually hear it was more awful, still.

"Yes. You should know that he did *try* to fight for you, but I would not be budged."

Just as fast as her heart had sunk, it felt as though it had snapped back into place. Even though Ives had spoken the words in a gentle tone, she couldn't help a flicker of agitation. "Why me, then? Why could you not find another like me? You said yourself there are others with the same blood."

"Because you're not *just* one of these people. We'd never have crossed paths unless you were the one *meant* for us."

"You were born for us to love you," Cassius said, his blue eyes swimming a bit.

"That's what you meant, isn't it?" She would ignore for now the way she felt to hear him speak of love, she had to. Her emotions were all over the place and she was just as likely to give in to them— to give in to *whatever* they wanted of her—before having her answers. "When you said it's not as simple as merely taking their blood? It's love, isn't it? You need to *genuinely* love them."

"And we do. We have from the moment you heard my story and still agreed to stay and help me. Your compassion and your patience, day after day—I'd never seen anything like it. Except, perhaps, from Ives."

Violet didn't know if they'd sidetracked from her initial question, or were leading up to it *eventually*. "Let's circle back to this business about me inviting you?"

"Your first night here," Ives said, shrugging against her, "we awoke, each of us, to you standing outside our doors. You led us back to your room, and then, well, you remember the things which happened next. The following morning, the marks were gone, we knew it was your blood at work. Yet, you seemed oblivious to what had gone on. The *Sanguinem Aeterna*, it is said, are supposed to come into an understanding of who and what they are when confronted with the ones meant to be theirs. We thought at first you were ashamed, or that perhaps you were trying to maintain some veneer of professional boundaries during the day to keep up the guise of propriety—to have what you could be to us and what your post in the household was entirely separate. You were so very fixated on station.

"After the first few times, however, we understood that you were unaware of what you were doing at night. When you spoke to me of the dreams you were having, I knew that your mind was working to shield you from the truth. We abstained for days after that, but then you began coming to us, again."

"We allowed you little peeks at us during private moments. Let you overhear our conversations in hopes it would be the smoothest way to jog your memory. What you feel for us is the catalyst, though. Our love counts for nothing without yours. We thought . . . ." Cassius uttered a chuckle filled with self-derision, then. "We *stupidly* thought you had loved us as easily and as readily as we loved you."

"But I do love you." The sentence fell from her lips faster than she could stop it, but the look of devotion in Cassius' eyes as he heard those words made her certain she wouldn't take back her confession even if she could have. "Both of you. I've been so confused. So . . . tormented. I didn't understand how I could love both of you like this."

"You really do?" He stepped closer, slipping one hand from hers to cup her jaw. "You *love* us?"

Violet's lower lip trembled as she stared into his eyes. "So much it hurts my heart."

"You've known what we are for some time now, haven't you?" Ives asked.

She nodded. "I wouldn't let myself believe, but I suspected, yes."

"Yet, you only tried to run away now?"

"I didn't *want* to leave; for weeks I'd agonized about it. I'd risk thinking my sanity was slipping, I'd risk scandal, I'd risk a mad specter wandering the corridors just to stay here with both of you. But when I actually saw the evidence of what you are with my own eyes, I suddenly feared you *would* hurt me, after all."

"Violet, you lovely and exasperating creature. Don't you know?" Cassius leaned closer, still, so close she could feel the coolness of his bare skin through the coarse fabric of her dress. "Ives said we would never, but what he should've said is that we *could* never. You're our heart. And you have been since the moment you walked into our lives."

She could feel that there were tears rolling down her cheeks—why hadn't she realized sooner how important she was to them? Not only her blood, not merely her body, but her. Her mind, her feelings, even her constantly fluctuating reliance on logic. *All* of her.

Isabeau's message . . . . It hadn't been a warning, at all. After her death, every word ever spoken about Isabeau Mercier's final months of life had been a lie. Dishonesty had denied her the history she deserved as a woman protecting the one she loved.

That was her message. For Violet to stop lying to herself. To be honest. To live freely.

Cassius brushed away her tears with the backs of his knuckles as Ives hugged her tighter, still.

"Stay, please. You can exist with us *always* as you are now. All it would take is a taste of our blood, but we won't force you." Cassius' lower lip poked outward in an expression that was almost a pout as his gaze searched hers. "Violet Ramsey, say you'll be ours forever."

Chapter Eighteen

The Question of Eternity

"If I take your blood," she began, curious as to how she managed to find her voice with Cassius' eyes so steady on hers like this, full of emotion as they were, "wouldn't that make me a vampire, too?"

"No. Because of what you are, you'd remain human. *Eternally* human."

She could feel a heavy warmth pressing on her chest as she considered the matter. It wasn't a burdening weight, more that it was oddly calming. A strangely lulling sensation, keeping her wholly at ease as she thought. Violet couldn't deny that her memories of them feeding on her blood had become sweet, treasured glimpses to her. Intoxicating, really. And the idea that they could, again and again, with no harm to her?

There was a faint flicker of jealousy through her as she recalled Ives' mention of taking the blood of vagabonds to sustain themselves, despite that she'd not even been part of their lives, yet.

"And you—neither of you—would need to feed on anyone else's blood ever again?" Her voice came out a bit breathless, and she wondered if her tone betrayed that she already knew what her answer was.

"Precisely," Ives replied, dipping his head to brush his lips against her throat.

Her eyes drifted closed and she found herself leaning back in Ives' embrace. "You expect me to think when you do such distracting things?"

"I was under the impression you were finished thinking on this," he said, slipping his hands back up along her sides and to her neck to start tugging at her dress.

"And I that you rather welcomed 'such distracting things' from us by now," Cassius tacked on, that familiar, wicked half-grin of his curving his mouth.

"But wait, wait . . . ." She shook her head in a slow, wobbling manner. "If you can only sustain yourselves on human blood, why did you bite Ives?"

She could feel the rush of breath against her skin from Ives exhaling an airy laugh as Cassius grinned. "Oh, that. That's simply because I enjoy the sensation of my teeth sinking into flesh, which Ives graciously obliges."

Opening her eyes, she met Cassius' gaze again. Violet needed to witness it once more. Needed to assure herself that now—now that they'd been completely forthright with her, and she with herself—what they were no longer frightened her.

"I want to see that again," she said, her voice barely a thread of sound as it spilled out.

She could swear she felt a small tremor wrack Ives' frame at her request. Well, that was interesting. It seemed that not only did Cassius enjoy the sensation of biting, but that Ives enjoyed being bitten.

"Ives?" Cassius lifted his gaze to the other man's. "Will you oblige me once more?"

Nodding, Ives raised one arm around Violet. As she'd seen earlier through the keyhole, he offered his wrist. Cassius returned his attention to the woman between them as he slid his hand around Ives'. Those blue eyes holding hers unflinchingly, he pulled back his upper lip, allowing her to watch as his canine teeth elongated.

To watch as he lowered his mouth to Ives' wrist and bit down, sinking those needle-sharp points into his lover's fair skin.

A small, choked-seeming gasp rumbled out

of her at the spectacle. She could feel Ives shuddering against her. She could hear a sound of bliss work its way out of him. And all the while, Cassius observed her, even as he nursed Ives' blood from the wounds he'd created.

Her skin flushed and there went that sweet clenching low in her body—the one that seemed edged by some mild aching.

They were so beautiful. They were creatures the world didn't believe existed. They *loved* her ... and she could literally stay with them forever.

"Yes," she said, that single word bursting abruptly in the quiet room.

Cassius eased his fangs free of Ives' skin as he stared at her. "You're truly certain? Say yes, again, and I'll share Ives' blood with you this very moment."

"Yes."

He didn't hesitate then. Taking another sip from Ives' wound, he lifted his head to capture Violet's mouth with his own.

There was a sense as though she were melting into him as she caressed his plunging tongue with her own. If he didn't know any better, he'd swear she was trying to lap up every last drop of Ives' blood in her eagerness.

She broke the kiss, wincing a little as she gave herself a shake. Already, she could feel something was ... different. She felt *more*. The fabric of her dress suddenly seemed rougher against her skin. More confining. The darkness further inside the house beyond the scope of the foyer lantern's illumination was nuanced now—where she only saw the shadowed recesses before, *now* she was able to discern shapes, furnishings and objects silhouetted against the greater darkness of the night.

Everywhere their skin touched hers, that chill was sharper, causing the contrasting heat of her own skin to spike. She understood, now. That had never been her imagination. Her body reacted to their coolness by keeping her warm.

Looking to Cassius, and then turning her head to look up at Ives over her shoulder, she felt her jaw go slack. They had somehow become even more breathtaking.

A bit of blood from one of them really *was* all it had taken.

In something of a daze as she tried to note every change she felt; whilst Ives' blood did its work awakening her, she became aware they'd been undressing her all this time, from the very moment that second *yes* left her lips. Her garments now pooled around her feet.

She could not to seem to take her eyes from Cassius lowering to his knees before her. Was the whisper of fabric behind her really Ives removing his dressing gown as Cassius saw to unlacing her boots?

As though in answer to her thoughts, Ives pressed against her, then. She bit her lip to hold back in a delighted sigh, adoring the feel of his cool, bare skin on hers. He smoothed his hands down along her sides before circling them forward and up, to cup her breasts.

Cassius, almost careless in that mischievous way he had, tossed her boots aside and assisted her to step out of the bundles of material on the floor. He held her leg, at last tearing his gaze from hers as he let his eyes drift closed and pressed a kiss to the inside of her ankle.

She thought surely she must be in another daze as she simply kept on, observing his reverent motions. His touch was so gentle, his lips impossibly soft as he kissed a path up along her leg. He paused at her knee, and she jumped a little at the touch of his other hand between her thighs. She'd been distracted by the delicate sweep of his lips, and Ives teasing her breasts.

"You truly want this? You want to be with us *completely*?"

Nodding, she slipped one hand over Cassius'. Recalling those evening glimpses, she guided his fingers into motion against her. "Completely."

Cassius nodded back, dragging his lips up along the inside of her thigh as he steadied her, bracing her leg over his shoulder and relinquishing his hold. The hand between her thighs stroked against her slow, but insistent.

"Tilt your hips back, darling," Ives, silent all this time, said in a low, gruff whisper in her ear.

Doing as he bid her, she felt the hardened length of him against her. But she was aware of a separate movement, too. She didn't have to look, she knew it was Cassius. Reaching his free hand up to stroke over Ives.

"Up on your toes."

Again, she followed his bidding. If not for Cassius before her, she was certain she'd have fallen over in a rather comical fashion. During that vaguely distracting thought, she braced herself, one hand back to grip Ives' bare hip, the other threading into Cassius' hair and curling into a fist.

A moan tore out of her as Cassius positioned him and Ives thrust his hips, entering her.

Though she froze as he withdrew and pressed forward a few times, there was the most delicious little shiver wracking her with each repetition. As Ives worked up to a rhythm, Cassius parted her, sealing his lips around the tender little bundle of nerves revealed.

Cassius lapped and suckled as Ives sank into her again and again, and Violet thought how stupid she'd been to almost walk away from this. They were *worshiping* her.

And she was going to spend eternity letting them.

But her inexperience was her undoing—she had no idea how to slow her body's response to their ministrations—and it wasn't long before she found release. Ives wasn't nearly finished, she could tell. His movements were steady, but sharper, harder as he felt her tightening around him. At the way her limbs stiffened, Cassius tilted his head this way and that, just as eager to help . . . nursing that sensitive little bead of flesh though her orgasm.

She screamed behind closed lips as her body gave out, rocking between them of its own volition as the blissful sensations ebbed.

Yet, no sooner had her orgasm started drifting from her than did she find them moving her. She didn't know how much more she could take when Cassius pulled away to sit on the floor. Ives lifted her entirely, withdrawing and then kneeling with her in his arms. She let out another of those horribly wanton moans as he lowered her over Cassius' lap, and she felt herself being filled anew.

Violet was cognizant Ives hadn't spent himself yet, but she adored knowing what they were to one another. Even as Ives' fingers gripped her hips to rock her against Cassius' motions, she took one of Cassius' hands in her own and guided it to wrap around Ives' still-hardened length.

"I trust you'll teach me how to do this?" she asked in a halting, exhausted whisper when she felt the motion of Cassius' arm as he followed her behest, working his hand over Ives.

"Oh, God, yes," Cassius answered with a chuckle.

Lowering his mouth, he kissed a path down to her breasts whilst they moved against each other. He knew what biting her just now would do, and so he held back for a time. Cassius' attention flicked from her face, her head tipped back a

203

little and her lips moving in silent prayers as Ives rocked her over his thrusts, to Ives' face above her shoulder. His teeth were sunk into his lower lip and his eyes were closed in the most exquisite expression.

When he found himself nearing that edge, Cassius tightened his grip on Ives a little. The other man opened his eyes, meeting Cassius' gaze. "Violet?"

She only managed a whimpering moan in acknowledgement of her name.

"We're going to feed from you now."

Violet nodded to Cassius' words, suddenly feeling as though she'd been waiting this entire time for them to do exactly that.

She felt those sharp pins—at her breast from Cassius, at her throat from Ives—but the pain was fleeting, as it always was. Soon there was nothing but the sweetness of them drawing from her wounds, the feel of Cassius' length thrusting into her again and again, the awareness of him working Ives to release, and the sensation of their skin slowly warming against hers.

Throwing back her head, she let out an ecstatic scream as they brought her to orgasm once more. She could hear the rough groan that rumbled low in Ives' chest as he fed from her whilst finding his own release. Cassius' motions became sharper and unsteady, until he stilled against her, spending himself as Ives' guidance kept her rocking over him.

Everything slowed by increments until they had each finished. Until they were each shuddering and thoroughly drained.

Violet all but collapsed between them as they withdrew their fangs. All three struggled to steady their breathing, but no one moved to disentangle themselves from the other two.

After what seemed forever, she said in a shocked whisper, "Oh, my Lord. I'm so embarrassed."

Both vampires pulled themselves from their blissful, languid stupors to give her quizzical looks.

She glanced from one to the other, and back. "Well, Gilbert lives here, too. What if he walks in on us like this? We *did* just make a bit of a racket."

Cassius burst out laughing as Ives hugged her from behind. "You're adorable, you are. Gilbert's a total recluse. Never leaves his room in the servants quarters unless we summon him, or he has a particular task at a particular time of day."

"It's why we hired him. Shut-ins don't ask a lot of questions so long as they can mostly be left alone."

"Oh." She pursed her lips. Not that she actually wanted to discuss Gilbert just now, but while they were on the topic . . . . "I've been wondering about something. On the subject of Gilbert, I mean. *How* is he so strong?"

"Of course, it should've occurred to us you would ask." Ives shrugged. "It's what happens when a regular human partakes of a nip of vampire blood."

"Well . . ." she said, nodding, but left it at that, having no idea what more to say.

"We give him a few drops every now and again to add to his food or drink."

"And he doesn't raise any questions about that?"

"It's hardly as though we *tell* him it's our blood. He knows it's a substance that keeps him vital and makes him stronger than any ordinary man has the right to be. So, he doesn't bother with curiosity on the matter."

She nodded again, glad her own curiosity on the matter had so simple an explanation. Well, as much as anything to do with vampires living in an estate once haunted by the ghost of a murdered witch could be considered *simple*, of course.

For several heartbeats, the three lapsed into silence. Violet breathed a content sigh, loving the way Ives was holding her. Loving the way Cassius leaned over her to press his lips to the other man's before he dropped a gentle kiss on her forehead and then rested his head on her shoulder.

"So . . ." she began in a whisper, breaking the quiet, "every night will be like this?"

"Yes," Ives said, his voice pitched gorgeously low.

Cassius tacked on with a note of pure mischief, "Well . . . days, too, if you like."

"You two *are* trying to kill me, I knew it!"

They each laughed at her facetious accusation, both tightening their hold on her.

∞∞∞∞

She must've drifted off at some point, she realized, because she awoke in her own bed. The sun streamed in through the window and she blinked, for a moment in fear that she'd dreamed all of that.

Except that as she snuggled beneath her covers, still quite worn out, she was greeted by the pleasant press of barely-warm skin on either side of her. Pillowing her head in the hollow of Cassius' shoulder, she closed her eyes again and wriggled herself back a bit against Ives' solid form curved behind her.

"Watch that, darling. None of us will get any rest you keep that up."

A grin curved her lips at Ives' rough, sleepy whisper in her ear.

Cassius chuckled, shaking his head against the pillow. "Troublemaker we've found ourselves."

"Troublemaker you've got on your hands forever," she pointed out, snuggling tighter between them.

Ives made a satisfied rumbling sound in the back of his throat as the other vampire said, "Oh, we're aware. And those are the happiest words we've ever heard."

Epilogue

A Scandalous Forever

C assius arched a brow as Violet came into the study with a missive in hand. Her expression was strangely unreadable.

Exchanging a glance with Ives, he asked, "What's that you've got there?"

She pursed her lips in thought as she looked up at them. "Reminder from Grace, Fletcher's fiancée, about the wedding. It's in just a few weeks. Apparently, she's afraid the country air has addled my brain and I might forget."

Cassius eased himself out of the armchair

before Ives' desk and crossed the room to stand before her. "Addle *your* brain? Hah, as if anything could."

She accepted the compliment with a gracious half-nod.

He cast a quick glance toward Ives, who only watched them with a feigned wariness. "That's not what the expression on your face is about, though, is it?"

"No." She gave a wry half-smile as she shook her head, handing him the missive to read for himself. "She's asking if I'll be attending unescorted. I think she's looking to match me up."

"Well, we can't have that," Ives said with a frown, his voice stern.

"We most certainly can't," she agreed as she took the missive back and turned on her heel to start back out of the room.

"Where are you off to now?"

"To my room to write my response. I'm going to inform her that I'll be bringing *two* guests with me."

"Two?" they asked in unison.

Pausing in the doorway, she looked back at them over her shoulder. "Certainly. You'll *both* be escorting me, of course."

"You realize that's going to raise some eyebrows?"

She turned back just a bit at Ives' question, a grin curving her mouth. Since the night she'd taken his blood, he dared say she had developed a mischievous streak that nearly rivaled Cassius.' "What's a little scandal *now* when we have forever?"

Violet disappeared from the doorway, and Ives merely stared after her. He didn't know whether to laugh or scratch his head. "I do believe we've created a monster."

"Oh, yes." Cassius said, meeting Ives' gaze with that playfully wicked smile of his. "Makes me love her all the more."

"Strangely? Me, too."

Throwing himself once again into the chair, Cassius let his head fall back, his tone wistful as he said, "Eternity's going to be fun."

The End

Acknowledgements

I don't normally do an acknowledgments page, simply because my novels have kind of been one-woman-shows. I give a nod to important people in my life, or those who aided in any way in the dedication, and that's usually it, but I thought just because I'm putting this out into the world by myself doesn't mean I'm alone.

So here we are.

I *warmly* acknowledge the fanficiton community. You get chided and dismissed far too easily by outsiders who make no attempt to understand what it's actually all about. In that community, I've found lifelong friends (especially my girls, Ellie, Melody, Jessi, and Mary), and I found my voice. Without the support and love I found there, I don't know that I'd have the courage to publish a darn word. With that, there's also an acknow-ledgement to my husband, Daniel, who has be-lieved in and supported me from the first moment I said I wanted to be a writer.

The last mention is less personal, but *just* as important. To the contributors on iStock-photo.com, whether you merely had an eye for a great shot, or created some wonderous feat of digital art, you've enabled writers and other art-ists to more fully realize their own visions and present them to the world. You don't get nearly enough credit.

Other Books by Gerilyn Marin

The Graced Girl

After suffering head trauma as a child, Camille Joubert finds herself existing amongst a hidden world of modern-day elves. Though she's not the only one of her kind, being best friends with their prince does bring its fair share of disruption to their lives.

Not everyone in Camille's changed existence is particularly happy to have a 'savage' human in their midst.

Blood and Fire (An Alpha Females Novel)

Newly-turned werewolf Imogen Cross finds her-self leading a pack that's members would rather kill one another than cooperate. Well, when they aren't tearing into each other in an entirely differ-ent way, that is.

If she can get them to keep their hands off one another long enough to come up with a plan, they might actually survive encountering the beast coming for them.

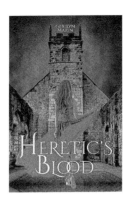

Heretic's Blood

A haunted campus, an abandoned church, a kid-napping, an obscure, long-forgotten blood cult, and a secret romance with a childhood friend-turned-enemy?

And here Melody Bennett thought her freshman year at Dorning University would be boring.

Witch-Child (The Salem's Refuge Trilogy, Bk 1)

Everything in 'barely psychic' high school senior Cae's life is as normal as can be expected when you grow up in a town that has no idea it's forgotten its own history and brushes off paranormal phenomena on account of how often it happens.

Until she gives in to her curiosity about the new boy in town.

Cloak of Crimson (An Adult Fairy Tale Novelette)

Would-be huntress Amia Lyfing will do whatever it takes to get the upper hand against Marrok Bleddyn, the werewolf lurking in the forest near her village. As it happens, 'whatever it takes' turns out to mean donning a cloak bespelled to lure out males of his kind.

She has no idea the cloak is just a pretty piece of fabric and that the thing which will draw Marrok to her is within her blood.

Printed in Great Britain
by Amazon